Interstellar

Epiphany

This book is a work of fiction. All persons portrayed belongs to a probable future. Although the events depicted may be probable, they are carried on by improbable persons.

Cover design by Sal Godoïj

Book design by David MacDonald

Printed by KDP, an Amazon.com Company
ISBN: 9798594284319

Interstellar Epiphany

Sal Godoïj

As I was snoring on my pillow, oblivious of the rest
A flashing serpent's tongue flickered in my window,
silhouetted me at best
I was dreaming something about rainbows,
something about sunsets
But then, my Alter Ego
Exuded through my pores, like perspiration I never sweat
Flowed out of my eyes, like tears I never shed
Came out of my ears, like words I never heard
And seized my dream
I wanted to wake up and could not
He forced my eyes shut, kept my mouth mute
Held my body immobile as if I were dead
"I am not a dream!"
Thundered my Alter Ego's flickering serpent's tongue
"I come from where you come."
"I am who you are and who you will become."
He pulled me out of bed, showed me no pity
A flash of lightning silhouetted us both
Scrambling together as under oath
Over the roofs we went, over the city
A heartbreaking symphony flooded space
And all of a sudden, like an epiphany, it was all on my face
That which avoids the eyes, although the eyes are open
That which avoids the mind, although the mind is open
That which avoids the ears, although the ears are open

And I learned about him, who is the other me, within me
And about my neighbours' fortune,
grace, disgrace, and misfortune
I was no longer I
I cast away my knowledge, fears, sins, hopes,
and God as well.
Like cockroaches hiding in the night,
my lies died haunted by the light
A flashing serpent's tongue flickered in my window
Weeping in my dream, restless on my pillow,
silhouetted me the gleam
A lightning whip my skin lashed, my heart scarred,
my soul slashed
"Wake up now!"
Thundered my Alter Ego's flickering serpent's tongue
"Like the wind that propelled forward the first ships
go about the Earth!"
"Free all men from their condemnation."
"Become the lightning that their dreams flash."
"Be the whip that their knowledge lashes."
"And their fears, sins, hopes, and God as well."
"Bring their truths out of the night."
"Bring their lies out to the light."
"Now and ever, and for the times forever."

The Dreamer, by Sal Godoïj

EARTH AND IT'S MOON

Source: The Earth Observatory. EOS Project Science Office at NASA Goddard Space Flight Center. The NavCam1 from the Origins Spectral Interpretation Resource Identification Security-Regolith Explorer -OSIRIS-Rex captured this image on January 17, 2018, at 64 million kilometers (40 million miles) from the Earth.

It's about your transcendence that I'm here

Human's absolute transcendence is what I'm bringing back

In exchange

Leave behind every ephemeral satisfaction you nurture

They are

The Homo sapiens' damnation

Axumeriedes, page 21

TOUCHDOWN

THE FIRST alert came from an amateur astronomer. The unidentified object was high in the sky. It could have been a shooting star, but it did not disappear into the night. Instead, it became brighter as it was approaching the Earth. And it was approaching fast, yet none of the space agencies were shedding light on this event.

People could see it now in daylight. It hovered over the city, for it seemed that it had chosen the city as its place of landing. Being closer to the strange object caused the citizens to fall into a state of general hysteria. Everybody could see it now with the naked eye, although no one could yet define what it was. It was shining up there. It had no known physical shape. It was not that big, though, and the comparison in size to a big bus remained in the citizens' minds. It shone like a star. It shone so much that it was difficult to stare at it with naked eyes at some point. This object above appeared to be shapeless, weightless. If it were a machine, what kind of machine could it be? Scientists wondered what could be keeping the device shining and moving with such ease.

Cameras broadcasted the image of this shining object to all four points of the globe.

The object stopped in midair above the city center and stood there for a long time. Warplanes and helicopters were already in the air, yet none of them approached the object. They circled it at a prudent distance. The UFO bounced and soundlessly moved. The speed at which it moved created the illusion that there was not one but many of these objects. It seemed to be in several places simultaneously, toying with the warplanes, while down in the city, curiosity became panic.

Then, everything happened. The object leaped into the lake along whose banks the founders had built the city. A bright, straight line slashed the city skyline, broke at a sharp angle, and went down into the lake. The entire lake seemed to boil at the impact. For an instant, a sphere, like a soap bubble, floated over the troubled water. And like in a soap bubble, the city skyline reflected in its bright external walls. The sphere submerged, and the water was calm again. Everyone raced to the lakeshore.

When it was all calm, the figure of a man rose from the water. Naked, the man waded ashore, carrying a large fish in his hands — the aquatic creature was wriggling high above his head.

The view awed the multitude. Miracle! It is a miracle! This thought was in everybody's mind. It could have been a miracle, for the sight of a live fish in the lake's polluted water was but a distant memory to most citizens.

Before reaching the beach, the man turned around. With a delicate motion, he released the fish back into the water. Then, he faced the crowd gathered on the beach — the citizens. The citizens held in their hands every recording device they had. Everyone struggled to get a close-up of the stranger. Several TV channels were there, their teams ready to report the news. Authorities from all levels of government were present as well. The police cordoned off that part of the lakeshore. Expecting action, a section of the military headquartered in the zone came as well, the soldiers dressed in full combat gear. The noise made by people and machines was unbearable.

In seconds, the news was all over the world. The prime minister was in constant communication with other world leaders. A UFO had landed, and we were about to have the first contact ever with an extraterrestrial. Yet, there was no sight of the UFO, the vehicle that brought the strange man to that location. The water of the lake looked calm and silvery. There were no signs of having ever suffered the impact of any foreign device.

The man stood on the beach, his bare feet lapped by the tide of the lake. He raised his right hand as if he was going to wave, but he did not. He held it up there, immobile as if not knowing what to do next. He kept his left arm pressed at the side of his body. He did not smile. He was observing everything and everybody with genuine curiosity. At a prudent distance, the citizens formed a half-circle around him. Those who stood further behind strained to have a better view of the man. Some of them were standing on their toes, peeping over or around the shoulders of those in front. Who could this man be?

The stranger was a replica of the male figure in the plaque placed on board the Pioneer 10 — NASA's spacecraft in 1972. Even his hair was the same length and combed in the same style. Could this likeness to the man in the plaque be but a mere coincidence?

Several hypotheses ran through the minds of the onlookers. He could be a pilot from an enemy nation. He was flying an unknown device and crashed while spying on us. But why would he appear naked before us all? It was not possible. No pilot on Earth would have presented himself in such a natural outfit and to such a gawking crowd. Nor did he seem to hurt after such a violent landing. And if the man was an extraterrestrial being, his appearance was, as said, that of an average male human being. He did not look tired after that allegedly unusual extended cruising through deep space. A fortyish something man, he was tall, but not much more so than your regular six-foot or so neighbour. He was muscular, but again, similarly to many others who practice some sport. Other than that, the man was far from what everybody thinks an extraterrestrial being should look like. Yet, he could have been using his human appearance to deceive people, or he was a sensitive extraterrestrial who did not want to scare the children.

On the machine's nature that fell into the lake, no one knew a thing about it yet. Nobody knew if it was, in fact, a spaceship, a device, or some other kind of contraption. It could as well have been a piece of a dead star or a fragment of a meteorite. Or was it not a spaceship, but a bubble, traveling on radio wavelengths generated by the stars? Or he may have come down to Earth on a flying carpet, for that matter. After all, we all should have paid more attention to fairy tales. From this perspective, they would not have been as enchanting as they were when we read them as children. And so, the crowd seemed to enjoy gobbling down on a banquet of speculations.

By then, everybody stared at the naked man, who held them at a distance with the strength of his serene demeanor.

The multitude waited. Some of the onlookers turned their backs to the man and wriggled out away from the scene. They were the skeptics. They suspected a hoax. A hidden marketing power, using them all as a frame for the promotion of a new product. It would not be the first time. There is always room for imagination.

"Do you speak English?" someone cried.

Other cries followed. "What language do you speak?"

"Who are you?"

"Where do you come from?"

There was no answer from the man. His appearance aroused the curiosity of the populace even more. Indifferent to all, the man stood there in silence. He seemed comfortable, though, surrounded by the frantic multitude.

A line of soldiers ran along the first line of spectators. They knelt in front of the crowd, placing their sight and weapons on the stranger. The mob grew restless. Nobody knew what was going to happen. The atmosphere became electric.

And then, the man stepped onward toward the multitude. They all paid attention. Those who were leaving turned around to retake their lost spaces. At the man's first step, the soldiers stood up and mounted their rifles from their ready position. Pushed by their routine, the TV crews adjusted their cameras. The photographers followed suit. The radio announcers and TV presenters described the scene.

What happened next, no one expected. It all became a bizarre scene — an absurd dance. The man moved a step forward, and the crowd moved a step backward. The soldiers followed the swinging of the mass. The man stopped, and the multitude stopped. But then, because the man stopped, the crowd, as if on cue, again moved a step forward. And then, the naked man advanced a step onward, and everybody moved a step backward. The strange dance went on for about ten minutes or so until the man stood still. With one foot in the air, he seemed to reflect on his next move.

Motionless, the crowd waited in silence. And as if indeed it were a game, the man stepped forward, and in a few strides, reached the first line of onlookers.

Caught by surprise, the mob opened a path for the naked man. He walked through with a self-possessed gait. While he walked, he watched the multitude with gentle curiosity. Then he fixed his sight on the skyscrapers. He was walking toward the city. The helicopters swirled up there, yet the crowd's buzzing reduced the humming of their rotors to a murmur.

People were praying. Others were crying hysterically, hitting themselves in the chest, kneeling, or screaming.

"He's Jesus! He's Jesus!"

"Aw! He's no, Jesus!"

"He might be!"

"He's an extraterrestrial!"

"He's not an extraterrestrial. Extraterrestrials are little green men with a big head and bulging eyes!" replied an informed child.

A choir was singing a psalm at full volume, and a riot was taking place a few blocks away. The police were charging the rioters in full force. The citizens continued to give vent to their feelings.

"He's the Lord!"

"Give praise to the Lord!"

One block away, a group of vandals had set a bus on fire. Further down, another fire started on the ornamental trees. The fire took off with force, and several roofs were now burning. The poignant smell of the smoke and the pepper gas used by police upset the multitude. As the riots were spreading out in a ripple effect, so was the fire. Parked cars began to burn. The crowd moved around as trapped horses do in a corral. A rain of stones fell on the police. The clamor of the multitude grew stronger. Several groups formed. Debates grew in length, depth, and format.

"He is a pilot that has lost his spacecraft and his uniform."

"He is a prophet of God."

"He is but a man."

"They are filming a movie but just won't tell us."

"I recognize him to be a neighbour."

"He is a relative of a friend…"

Indifferent to the commotion, the man strode in a straight line towards the city. His head high, his eyes fixed on the crowd, that like a wall, circled him. Some people tossed some garments for the man to cover his nakedness. The man did not attempt to grab them and continued walking. The garments left a path of colour at the man's step and then disappeared, trashed by the crowd's feet. The citizens had left their vehicles behind. On foot, like a tide, the mass followed the naked man, cheering all kinds of slogans and chants. It seemed as if a famous rock star had landed.

The man reached the city's outskirts, passed through the workers' shacks, and left behind the factories' line. A line of chimneys stood at his back. Behind him were the clanging and banging, cutting and hammering, and a thousand other noises of an industrial city. He passed the quarters of the rich and reached the city centre. The city centre was also in chaos. Radical groups took the streets and set barricades on fire to interrupt traffic. Those who wanted to live in peace, watch TV, and be merry could do none of these things.

TV and radios urgently summoned all kinds of experts in astronomy, extraterrestrial life, and space probes. The experts were now outpouring their knowledge, commenting on the interstellar visitor in front of a mesmerized audience.

The fires and the riot did not subside. The smoke now covered the city's downtown in a thick and chemical fog. The National Guard took control of the area. Cameras and other devices registered every image, which through the TV channels and on the internet, turned several times around the Earth.

More people arrived. They did so en masse, and the city could barely contain them all. Pilgrims who had come in caravans now populated parks, plazas, streets, and every space mushroomed with tents. Social media had a frenzy of exchanges on the event. The strange man stood by a park and watched the action that happened around him and because of him. He was calm and collected and had the look of a marveled child in his wide-open gray eyes.

The city lived its most vibrant day in decades. Every store, every pub, every market crowded beyond the legal limit. The airport's movement was ceaseless as it had never been before, and the same happened on the highways that crisscrossed the city. The prime minister, however, worried about such an unusual siege of his city. It has never seen it before. His concern focused on the needs that large gatherings bring.

Shelters for the pilgrims, for instance. And hygiene, water, food, and portable public toilets. Besides these issues, vandalism worried him as well. And so did an increase in other crimes.

The day was cold, but the people on the streets felt it to be the hottest and the best of their summer days.

AXUMERIEDES

A FEW HOURS after the stranger's arrival, the entire city looked like a camp invaded by an army of the homeless. People filled every single space around the man, who kept himself collected at all times. People carried flowers, banners made of every material, colour, and legend — and thousands of religious symbols of every kind and creed, flags, other ensigns, baskets, gifts, toys, and other presents intended to the messenger of the beyond, as a way to appease the gods. The expectant mass fell upon their knees and prayed. They kept their vigil, waiting for the man from beyond to speak to them.

Yonder, the mass became hysterical with the expectation that something would happen, and the disorder continued. A war tank entered the esplanade. At the sight of the massive war machine, people were horrified and ran, but then regrouped and came back to attack the tank. This action produced revolts that, at moments, became uncontrollable. Some people covered the tank's operator's vision with their clothes, and the war machine went in circles, endangering everybody around.

An officer of the army came to talk to the people, but

nobody listened. The officer left. The interstellar traveler man, surrounded by the multitude, stood there, impassible, watching every action. Neither the crowd nor the police or the soldiers came near him, for a kind of invisible electric aura surrounded the man. The soldiers vacated the area and made room for the authorities to go near to talk to this man. The prime minister was there with his cabinet and congress members and the media, the military, and various religious leaders.

Yet, the chaos persisted.

The soldiers who were on guard shielding the authorities suffered the most, struggling to remove the vociferating crowd, which threatened everybody's safety. An armed soldier stood every two metres, forming a large ring around the man. A backup guard covered a quarter of the esplanade. Yet, the military could not contain the riots. It threatened to reach dangerous levels, and if the situation persisted, it could end up as generalized social unrest. The smell of smoke brought by the wind from the fires and the police tear gas bombs was nauseating.

The tank in the esplanade was now burning. Molotov cocktails fell on it, and the flames caught the banners and flags that covered the tank. The fire expanded, causing alarm from those who were around it. A group of soldiers rushed to put down the fire with extinguishers. The burning war machine moved with a disturbing screeching sound, and the panicked crowd screamed. The tank left the area, and the screeching sound dimmed amongst the cheering of the people that continued to throw objects at it.

And yet, despite all this convulsion, the strange man

remained collected, standing there, now surrounded by thousands of people. His eyes surveying the crowd —his demeanor
impacted the multitude like the invisible force that kept them
all prudent distance from him.

 The prime minister looked at his watch and conversed with
an assistant. They could barely hear each other because of
the commotion that never stopped. The crowd cheered with
a passion that the ground shook and the air broke in waves
of despair, for it was a despairing crowd those who gathered
there.

A group of men brought a sturdy wooden picnic table, the
kind commonly found in parks, and placed it there, so the
guest from space would stand out on a stable higher level if he
wanted to address the multitude, as he seemed he was preparing to do.

Everybody was expectant of what was going to happen.
Two women came through the first line of onlookers and
advanced toward the man, fearless. The women's presence cut
the tension and transformed it into curiosity. The naked man
moved toward them and leaned in to pay attention to what
they had to say. It was the first-ever human contact with a
possible alien, and all cameras recorded it.

One of the women held a garment in her right arm. It was
but an ordinary ankle-long hooded monk's habit. Its coarse
fabric was the colour of ash. The two women offered the robe
as a present for the man, and he accepted the gift. The women
directed the man as to how to wear the garment. The man put
the garment on. Satisfied, expecting nothing else from the man,
the two women returned to their place within the multitude.

Reporters of all media pursued the two women. They had

questions about their gift to the strange man. They were
members of a theatre company, the women said. Both women
were costume designers working on a production, and they
heard about the naked man from space on their car's radio. It
happened that they had this garment in their vehicle, a leftover
of one of their recent productions, and decided to bring it up
to the man.

Now dressed in the monk's habit, the man stood up on
the table and surveyed the people. He raised his hand with
the same gesture of goodwill that the man in the Pioneer 10
plaque shows. The crowd cheered. Yet, despite his human
look when naked, wearing the monk's habit, the man looked
now more like Axumeriedes, a character from a TV series on
mystical events popular in the beginning of the 21st century, a
monk from an obscure monastery in the ancient city of Axum,
Ethiopia. Axumeriedes, —son of Axum — as in the Greek
spelling of his name. The quick wit of the crowd baptized the
stranger as Axumeriedes.

And thus, Axumeriedes addressed the multitude.

ON THE HOMO SAPIENS

It's about your transcendence that I'm here

Human's absolute transcendence is what I'm bringing back

In exchange

Leave behind every ephemeral satisfaction you nurture

They are

The Homo sapiens' damnation

You throw pebbles into a still lake

You do expect someone to notice those ripples

You want someone out there in the vacuum to answer you

Yet, the response may come

Are you ready to receive the response from the space out there?

I have seen what happened here in this one city upon my arrival

I assure you, you are not ready to receive visitors from beyond

And even so, you persist in sending probes

You even think to send crews into deep space

Exploring other worlds

Yet, I assure you that beyond your frontier

Beyond the Earth, there do exist those who wonder

Who are those who dare to disturb the peace of the space?

I noticed the ripples lapping at the shores of my world

And came to this planet to read your minds, to investigate your kind

In your past, others have done as well

They came here, landed on this planet, contacted you, yet you never contacted them

They left questions behind. They took the answers along

Others may follow, yet, be aware

You may not want to become the subject of unhealthy curiosity

Sending spaceships to interstellar space seems to be, for you, an extraordinary achievement

It might be an extraordinary achievement for your kind, yet, it is inappropriate

Reconcile yourselves with the Earth, instead

Use the synergy of hearts to improve yourselves

Surge forward and grow away from the Homo sapiens

Stop being larvae, and become the butterflies you should be

Do not ever look back, for no butterfly has ever returned to its chrysalis state

People had set their camps in every possible space they could find. Religious leaders gathered their flock and commented on Axumeriedes' every word, and spiced their comments with their perception of the teachings.

"Even though he might not be a human," said one of these religious zealots, "He is also a child of God."

"Amen," a choir responded.

"God is the Universe," commented another.

"The entire Universe is God's creation," assured another.

Indifferent to these comments and judgment, Axumeriedes continued his speech.

I bring a message to you

Humankind must become a different being

The crowd appeared edgy, uncomfortable.

The Earth is in danger, and you are in danger

The Earth will defend itself

You cannot defend yourselves

If the Earth doesn't defend itself, the cosmos will intervene

The Earth won't be another empty rock swirling around the star you call SUN

Nothing is new in the infinite spaces beyond

A species devouring their resources devouring themselves

And where was life before

Only dust remains

It is not a new happening. It had happened before

It is happening somewhere in the universe

The multitude wriggled in uneasiness.
"Is this guy threatening us or what? who does he think he is?"
The TV channels had mounted two large screens. The screens showed Axumeriedes in a close-up. In the background, the crowd, a flicking here and there, and the stern face of the prime minister.

The man they now knew as Axumeriedes continued speaking.

Crave for a harmonious life between you and the Earth

Far away, people continued arriving nonstop. The multitude now occupied the entire esplanade below, around the field where the military parade occurs during the country's national festivities, beyond the park that bordered the poor quarters' limits, and along the lakeshore.

The scientific community was present, as well. And so there

were the students, the philosophers, the priesthood, and the politicians. Axumeriedes had attracted people from all layers of society.

The news was already global. There were people from NASA and different organizations from Europe and Japan, Russia, and China. Many countries' secret services were there too, and diplomats, religious leaders, sects, gurus. All were active in the crowd and attentive to Axumeriedes' message. Axumeriedes spoke with authority. His voice, articulate, profound, and clear, reached every ear.

Fragile creatures, you are, frail is your society

What you do, whatever you do, increases your frailty

The unknown, darkness, the vacuum, takes you all

It shakes you all and dries you all of your energy

A fragile creation is your humanity

A few days without water, a few days without power, the outbreak of an unknown illness, a natural disaster, and you all, humanity, are in despair, in fear, in chaos

You get old, and when you get old, your body disavows you

Your memories fade away

You, who once was you, are no longer you, for life slices you with its sharpest knife

Time is life's sharpest knife

You must understand life because it is your responsibility

On Earth, life is your responsibility

You are going nowhere if you do not understand life

A minute sparkling dot in the infiniteness of space, the

Earth is

I have seen it from the remoteness of space

You would better understand my words if you could see the

Earth as I do

The crowd moved uneasy, restless.

You feel you are free

You are not free

You are prisoners who hope to be free

ON HOPE

I will tell you what hope is

Hope is a one-way road

You have but one exit

Hope should be now the quality of your past, not of the present, you live

It should never be a hope present in your future

You must not hope at the stage you are as humans because it shows how weak you are

You even hope for God to help you

But then, you hope, and this is wrong because you have never learned to choose

What hope can you find then in the wrong decision if said decision is yours and yours only?

Why then you claim for God and hope that He will rescue you from a situation you created?

For this is the way, The Principle built you

The sum of both parts, good and evil, gives you shape as humans; in action and reaction; that is all and nothing else

The sum of this all is what makes you humans, an exposed species

You are naked creatures struggling in the wilderness of events that you have created

You should never hope again because it reveals your weakness

Your immaturity as a species

But you persist in holding to this quality

Hope never comes free

There is no answer for your hope, neither from the outside nor the Heavens

The hope you speak about so freely comes from you, from within yourselves because it is alive, in you

You must learn to extract this hope from you

Give your hope a form

A shape

Give it an Absolute Human shape

Hope is wasted energy, and it weakens you

Parasite of your dreams is what hope is

A legacy you carry from your weakest period

You never knew, you never learned how to profit from it

Neither have you ever comprehended it, in its essence

Think, and act instead

Remember who your creator is

The Principle is

Your autonomy comes from The Principle

The Principle created you; abandoned you

You must dwell on this revelation until it pains you

For you are not free

Abandoned creatures are what you are

Incomplete creatures are what you are

Obsolete creatures are what you are

The crowd exploded in cries, and chaos resurged all over.
"What is this guy talking about?"
"Did he come here to judge us?"

ON THE ABSOLUTE HUMAN

A XUMERIEDES SURVEYED the multitude, and his voice raised, firm, clear, and decisive, dominating the noise, the cries, and the fear, and softened them all.

Civilization is what you call it, which is but the work of the confused Homo sapiens

You are behind where you should be because you do not know yourselves

Learn about yourselves first, then struggle to reach a real development

Learn about who you are, learn where you came from

Learn about the link between your roots and your role on Earth

Move on to the next stage

Achieve the metamorphosis of the Homo sapiens

Transform yourselves into the Absolute Human

The advanced species your creators expected you to become

Rise yourselves as a source of harmony among yourselves, the Earth, and the universe

There was a great commotion as some in the crowd started a fight. The fight spread out as in a ripple effect. The police tried to isolate passionate fighters. Again, Axumeriedes regained the harmony of his presentation.

Replace the human with the Absolute Human

The obsolete human is the Homo sapiens

The Absolute Human you must become

A different human will share the Earth

It will respect its kind

It will have a different view of the cosmos

A close-up of itself will signal the birth of the One Human, the Absolute One

Not different groups dispersed on the surface of the Earth

One Human, One Thought, One Earth

A new being on the Earth you must become

You must become the Absolute Human

Don't go into deep space as the Homo sapiens

What will the crew find when they return on Earth, but the Earth?

The way Homo sapiens has it, and even worse

Don't go into deep space as the Homo sapiens

Delay this cosmic ambition until you level yourself into one human

The Absolute One

Yet, once you level itself into one, there will not be a cosmic ambition

For the cosmos will come to you in the shape of wisdom

The Oneness' time, a better path for a better future to all on Earth

It will be but a painful process

Yet becoming better never comes free

Apocalypse, you call the end, but it is the beginning

It has started already, and it doesn't mean your extermination

Apocalypse is a transformative process, a sieve that you must pass through

Devastating, the origin of change is in you, and you only

Leave behind the Homo sapiens, climb the steps to become the Absolute Human

The entire Earth awaits your change

The Homo sapiens sets its life on ephemeral satisfactions

A tree with no roots, a sick tree; a tree that any small wind can tumble down

Become the Absolute Human

If you don't do, all efforts to project yourselves onward will be futile

You will always be dependent on your vices and, worst of all, on machines, and putting the planet at risk

You will be subspecies raised to feed machines, as you now raise cattle to feed yourselves

People's expectations grew, and their voices became thunderous.
   "What? How? What should we do?"
   Axumeriedes' demeanor dominated the anxiety his words provoked in the audience.

 As it happened before, it will happen again

I have seen it in other worlds, in other species, and in other minds

In deep space, there are no exceptions

You are not an exception

The Homo sapiens is part of your infancy as a species, the larva

Become the butterfly, transform yourselves

Mature as a species, leave the Homo sapiens behind

You are of a different kind, away from the nature of this
planet

You are artificial creatures made with a purpose you covered

Under the sand of your pride, your ignorance

Rediscover this purpose

Become worthy of the planet that gives life to you

Several voices rose from different points, words charged with
emotion and fear. Fear of the unknown, being the primordial fear,
very much present in modern humans. The police were hardly
trying to contain the overexcited crowd
  "How are we going to do it?"
  "How are we going to change?"
  Voices continued rising, the restless and anxious multitude
moved in waves, and the cries' intensity became deafening. For
over the chaos, reigned the calm, articulate voice of Axumeriedes.

Learn to know yourselves

What do you know about yourselves, about your inner
world?

You may think you know much, but you know little

You know little about the Earth, nothing about yourselves

What you have collected from your remote past are but

discarded versions of yourselves

I am not here to talk to you about an upcoming apocalypse that will sweep you all to extermination

I am here to tell you what you must do, for you are responsible for the future of the Earth

Keeping the Earth alive is your responsibility

Yet, to continue living on the Earth, you must change your thought, your vision, and your action

My words will be the last ones you will listen to from a messenger from deep space

What you will hear next will be but a proposition, yet it will not be a pleasant one

The roaring of the multitude became deafening.

"Are you threatening us or what?"

"Who do you think you are?"

"We have weapons to defend ourselves, dude."

"You are crazy, man!"

Riots restarted. Fires restarted. Fights ensued. The police effort struggled to contain the disorders. A group started a fire on a line of portable chemical toilets.

Yet, Axumeriedes did not mind the chaos around him. He had his eyes fixed on a point somewhere amid the multitude. Something was happening down there. Some people at the front line turned their heads to see what it was that attracted

Axumeriedes' attention, and what they could see was but an undulating sea of heads. Axumeriedes' eyes were but on one man. The man was jostling his way through, stepping forward toward where he was standing. Axumeriedes at once sensed the man's intention. The man had a handgun hidden in the pocket of his coat. He was fast closing the distance between himself and Axumeriedes, his intended target. His hand held tight on the grip of the hidden weapon.

But then, without hesitation, Axumeriedes came to his encounter. The multitude opened a path for him. Nobody knew what was happening. People started moving the way animals move when they sense danger, and then, there was a clearing in the crowd.

The man with the weapon reached the clearing, lifted his head, saw Axumeriedes standing there in front of him, yet he did not lose his coolness, and extracted the handgun from his pocket, aimed at Axumeriedes' chest, and pulled the trigger. Five quick blasts blinded those who were around. The noise made by the gunshots was deafening. Yet, there was no blood on Axumeriedes' chest. The failed assassin attempted one more shot, but then the weapon fell from his hand because he was shaking so much. Axumeriedes stepped on the gun, and the gun melted under his foot.

Axumeriedes faced the man and said,

You fear, then you hate, and you act. Stop! Fear and hate feed from your heart

And then, as if nothing had ever happened, he turned toward the multitude and said,

Share my words with those who will come to meet you with
a question in their eyes

He walked, and the crowd followed him as a caravan and were
thousands behind him.
The failed assassin dwindled, and no one paid attention
to him. The weapon was now but a fading stain on the dust.
On the road, witnesses recalled the murder attempt and how
Axumeriedes managed it.
"It's a miracle! It's a miracle!"

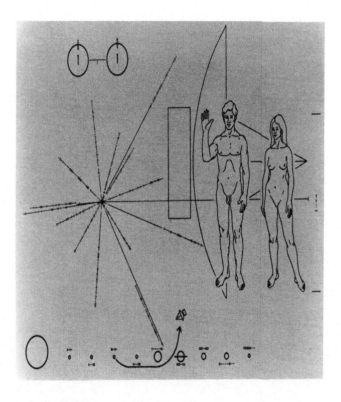

PARADOX

"I<small>T'S NOT</small> a miracle," said a teacher of a 12th graders class to his students. They were part of the crowd that followed Axumeriedes.

"Why do you say that, Mr. Lang?" one of the students asked.

"The said miracle could be but a deceptive subliminal projection, Sharon. All, for that matter, Axumeriedes, the light we saw, the fish in his hands, all seems to me to be a deceptive subliminal projection."

"Sorry, I don't understand, Mr. Lang," another student said.

"Look at him, Paul." The teacher responded. "Naked as he was, he didn't look like Axumeriedes. Unclothed, he looked like the human male figure we sent to space back in 1972 in the Pioneer 10 plaque."

"What do you mean, Mr. Lang?" the students asked in unison.

"It is obvious that somehow, they, the aliens, whomever they are up there, intercepted the Pioneer 10. Or the Pioneer 10 may have arrived somewhere, which explains Axumeriedes' analogy of us humans throwing pebbles into a still lake. Then, based on that male figure, they, the extraterrestrials whomever they are up there, copied our human features, and decided to come down here to investigate."

"They could have used the figure of the woman…" another student said.

"Yes, Mary-Jo, you may be right. They could, but they may know nothing about sex differences. They may have seen the figures as belonging to two different species. The man in the plaque is dominant, looks more conspicuous, and shows action. By contrast, the woman by his side looks static. Why did they make her look static? I don't know."

"You mean that she could have been waving her hand as well?" Mary-Jo asked.

"She could, Mary-Jo. But for us humans, this is a mere point of view. For the extraterrestrials, the whole thing may have had a different meaning."

"It was then a mistake to send that information, which tells too much about us?" another student asked.

"One thing is clear, Paul. If we want to communicate with extraterrestrials, we should leave behind our traumas."

"What do you mean, Mr. Lang?" another student asked.

"Axumeriedes said that we are what we have invented, Rachel."

"You mean, what we do believe we are?"

"Yes, Rachel. We are seeking for extraterrestrial life, and yet, we are aliens among ourselves."

The bustle and hustle of the crowd, moving, singing, talking, and praying, interrupted their conversation. Many persons carried diverse offerings, flags, banners, and simple cardboards with handwritten messages.

"Since the space race opened to competition," Mr. Lang

continued, "We have been playing expensive games teasing unknown forces."

"Are we in danger, then, I mean, as humanity?" Paul said.

"As Axumeriedes said it, we could be risking ourselves, opening our doors to an unhealthy curiosity."

"Whatever we have been doing, it has been to ensure the future of humanity," Sharon said.

"Not in a healthy way, Sharon. There is no doubt that the problems of our present are a legacy from our remote past."

There was another pause, demanded by the commotion caused by the marching crowd, now in a long caravan, yet no one wondered where Axumeriedes was taking them. He just walked ahead, greeting all those who came to receive him. He was already in the suburbs, entering the industrial area, with block after block of factories, abandoned warehouses, and then again, the shacks where poor people lived.

"And those that we will face henceforward," Mr. Lang said, to complete his idea.

"So, Axumeriedes is a time traveler," Paul said, trying to make his voice heard amidst the tumult. "He comes from the future, from here. From the same Earth."

"He looks like a human, yet you know he is not," Mr. Lang said. "Does he comes from the future? It's probable. But if he does, if he comes from the future, he is not from the Earth."

"I don't get it."

"In the Earth, we're always moving ahead, Paul," Mr. Lang said. "We cannot stop. Thus, time travel will be but a one-direction-only journey, always toward the future if it becomes possible. The paradox is that we cannot skip the present. To jump forward to a time in the future and come back. This paradox creates another: the only way we could see the future is through our past. Albeit, with imagination, study, and planning, this is what we do now, don't we? And if the answer is yes, then we all are passive time travelers."

"Are we?" the students asked in unison.

"This is the thing, ladies and gentlemen, the nature of time roots itself in the Earth's motion around the sun. Both rotation and revolution generate a gravitational force. This gravitational force generates a vacuum field, whose role is to act as a lubricant. It smooths the movement of Earth in space. This vacuum field is what we call time."

"So, time is a quality of mechanics, is it what you are saying?" another student asked.

"Yes, Patrick. And it acts as a measured force, like a hand squeezing an orange. Let's think that the Earth is an orange. It dries at every turn. Hence, the Earth and everything within it gets older."

"It seems hard to believe," Paul said.

"It is… indeed, Paul. Yet, it explains Enrico Fermi's Paradox

"How, Mr. Lang?" Rachel asked.

"Why in all these years, we have not seen any extraterrestrials before," Mr. Lang said. "The answer is: because of the time difference. The extraterrestrials live on another planet, and this is obvious to us. Which is not as obvious to us is that they live in a different time frame."

"What about Axumeriedes? He is an extraterrestrial." Patrick said.

"He found us. We didn't find him," Mr. Lang said.

"I'm not so sure about that, Mr. Lang," Paul intervened.

"Let me explain, Paul. Listen, class. Listen to my theory. The

extraterrestrials, whomever they are, must live in a time frame
either behind or ahead of us. Time, gravity, and light exist all
over the universe, albeit measured differently. And as I said,
time's nature roots itself in the planet's motion while moving
around its star. Then, the planet's motion generates a vacuum
within which it moves. If this doesn't happen, the planet will
remain static in space, and as a result, its internal forces will
cause it to explode. Its motion around its star tells us about the
planet's location, mass, and speed of movement, hence life,
weather, geography, and so on. Every planet is different. Thus,
at a different mass, different gravity, speed, motion, and so on.
Ergo, different timespan."

"But how does it work, Mr. Lang?" Sharon says.

"Take our historical events, for example, wars, pests, natural disasters, ancient civilizations. Let's say the Romans. They
existed here on the Earth; we do not doubt that. We have proof
of their existence. But they existed in a different period, which
we call "past." We cannot meet them anymore. To meet them
again, we must stop time, and we cannot do that. Likewise, we
don't see extraterrestrials because time, beyond distance, is
what separates us. And the same happens here on the Earth
as well, in our present time, of course. Let's say Australia, for
example. It is far away from us and in a different time zone.
Does this mean Australians don't exist? They do, of course,
they do carry on with their lives as everybody else does. But
if we want to meet them, say in a specific place and time, we
must agree on the meeting's location and time, and be punc-
tual as well, of course. If we don't do that, we will never meet.
And again, if we don't meet, it doesn't mean that they don't
exist. Is it not so?"

The students exchanged glances.

"Likewise, my dear students, the extraterrestrials are out there," Mr. Lang continued, "They do exist, as we do. Axumeriedes is proof of what I'm saying. The challenge then is to meet them, but if we aim to meet them, we must be both the extraterrestrials and us, in the same time frame. And this will only happen if we find an Earth-like planet, a replica of the Earth, in size, age, mass, rotational speed, distance from its star, and so on. Now you tell me, my friend. What are the chances of this happening among the millions and millions of planets out there?

"But then, how did Axumeriedes find us?" Paul said.

"He said how he did, Paul. He followed the thread left by the Pioneer 10. In other words, say that here on Earth, an anthropologist excavates a strange object. The object lies for thousands of years hidden under the sand of a desert. It turns out that the object is from another era, another civilization, but it is of an alien origin. We can do nothing about this in our actual state of development but to wonder what it means. I mean, to look at the sky with an interrogation sign in our mind and scratch our head. In an advanced society, they may decide to cross the barrier of time and distance. They have the means to come here and investigate, and it was what Axumeriedes did. They, the Axumeriedes of his world, have the means to travel through space and time. Because of the Pioneer 10, which they might have found buried in the sand of their desert, they have found us. They found the Earth, a world that is, of course, away from their time frame. Their preliminary observation might be that we humans are living in a remote past from them. And then, they must have found a way to move

on reverse through the Earth's lubricant vacuum, which, as
I said, we call time. They would have moved at will through
our past and present life. They would have done the way The
Principle he claims would have done hundreds of thousands of
years ago. An advanced species as they, Axumeriedes indeed
are, must have found a way to equal this feat. Or they may
have developed in their bodies a video-dimensional sensory
mechanism, a built-in superlative sense that would enable
them to see us not only in our present time but in our past as
well. They could have done that. The same way we do now,
watching a video of ourselves struggling to survive throughout
the times."

"But is this what he does?" Patrick said. "Does Axumeriedes
move outside of time?"

"I'm not quite sure about that, Patrick, but if he does so, the
most probable thing is that we are his dream."

"What?" the students exclaimed in unison.

"Yes, it is what I call a 'deceptive subliminal projection.' I
suspect Axumeriedes is dreaming about what is happening to
us now. We are in his dream."

"And we think it's real?" Rachel said. "It seems very real to
me."

"But how is that possible?" Paul said. "That we are part of
his dream?"

"Not yet at the actual stage of development," Mr. Lang said.
"But it is possible. No doubt about it, at least, in my mind. If
we could learn how to govern our dreams, that would be a
great advance. Then, we could travel through an induced
dream interface. Before we go to sleep, we set a destination
for our dream. Our body remains here, but our mind travels

through electrical waves. Then, our body materializes at the chosen destination. We could achieve to embody ourselves in another 'local' body as well. If we could do this, we can act independently of our regular biological needs. Think about it. We won't need oxygen because we aren't breathing from that atmosphere. Naked. No machines. Away from time and space. Only the legends of the natives of the world we visit will speak of us. And there will remain the monuments they would build under our direction, as a proof of our ever being there."

"This is incredible!" Mary-Jo exclaimed.

"Incredible things are happening in front of our very eyes," Patrick sentenced.

"Well," Mr. Lang said, "By learning to travel through deep space, we are creating paradoxes. How will this affect the mood of the crew in future spaceships is still a mystery."

"You mean, what did we learn from traveling to the moon?" Paul said.

"Right. We are still planning interstellar space travel using human-crewed spaceships. Why? Because an interstellar adventure will never be a success without us. We cannot send only robots and computers to our destination. The human presence is imperative."

"That's our human ego," Mary-Jo said.

"An ephemeral satisfaction, as Axumeriedes says, ladies and gentlemen," Mr. Lang said. "Yet, we measure distance in space as we do on Earth. Thus we use the same principles as flying within the Earth's atmosphere. We treat deep space as we have learned what it is: an emptiness between point A and point B. It might not be so. Space could be an elastic expanse that contracts and expands, like a great heart. And we do know that there are gases in space. These gases contract and expand. Besides the black holes, there must be currents we know nothing about yet. Yes, currents like in rivers and oceans. And there must be cracks through which we may fall in, like shortcuts to other worlds, to other dimensions. Look at him, Axumeriedes, not now, not tomorrow, but one day we will learn, and we will travel as he does. For him, now it is the real thing, but for us, it is still science fiction."

THE PRINCIPLE

THEY ARRIVED at a vast empty field. Axumeriedes halted, turned around, and saw the long line of people that followed him. The crowd gathered around him, the interstellar pilgrim standing there in all his authority. He seemed to have grown taller, or so was a general impression. Some people got near him and delivered him some gifts they had brought. Axumeriedes did not receive the gifts. He raised his right hand and said,

Every gift you give must go back to nature.

If it does not, then it is an offense to those who receive it, an offense to the Earth that sustains you

The crowd fell onto their knees, and Axumeriedes said,

Stand up, people

I am not a prophet sent by one of your gods

Yet I preach for your salvation, albeit not a heavenly one

I came here to talk to you about yourselves, about your origins

There is no renewal of the human species

There has not been a change of skin in the human being

You have been looking for the missing link in your species

There is a link between humans and animals, yet it is of a different kind

Axumeriedes made a long pause, and the multitude moved uneasy, expectant to his words. His voice came strong, stentorian, and clear to every ear.

In the beginning, animals and aquatic creatures, birds, insects, and spiders inhabited the world

Then The Principle came

And because of The Principle, humans beings roamed the Earth

In this order, male humans, then human females

Human life on Earth began with an experiment

The Principle

An extraterrestrial group

They came from a planet from which you do not have yet a reference

The Principle's home planet is twelve times the size of the Earth

Billions of years older than the Earth

The Principle's reproductive pattern is different from humans

They were not worried about genders

The Principle are human-like in appearance

The construction of their body is different, not comparable to humans

The Principle's body can adapt to physical forces yet unknown to humans

In the Earth's atmosphere

They can move from different levels of space-time

They have a different response to space-time challenges than humans do

They do not use machines to move from one space field to another

Time on the Earth is for them weightless

While on the Earth, no matter how many years go by, they do not change with time

For humans, time is a crushing condition to navigate through

The Principle are not the perfect angelical immortal beings you may imagine

They belong to an advanced race of individuals

They practiced their knowledge in the construction of a new creature on the Earth

You, the human being

The Principle explored the Earth, studied it

Experimented with a different kind of life

Man was born, Woman was born

The Principle knew about the male-female condition on the Earth

Yet, they did not set up a reproductive helix by creating male and female humans

For an unknown reason, their venture on Earth ended unexpectedly

They left the Earth. Hence, their experiment with human life ended, unfinished

You are the unfinished result of an impressive genetic technology, which is now obsolete

Hundreds of thousands of years obsolete

You, humans, are then the result of research, calculations, and studies made in a laboratory

The Principle improved their creature

They did so after a period of observing its behaviour and reactions

This way, this not-yet-human creature improved as it met new challenges

The Principle modified the creature's brain so that it could develop its proper tools

The primitive human became the penultimate model, which after the encounter with Woman, became the Homo sapiens, which is who you are now

At the dawn of your nature, The Principle did what you, at your present level of science and technology, do

You do testing with animals

You modify the environment to satisfy your ephemeral satisfactions

You build biological robots and experiment with artificial intelligence

It is what you do

You explore, destroy, build, destroy again, and abandon the place, leaving behind garbage as proof of your presence

Are there any ethics to your behaviour?

Killing each other in the most barbarous way, destroying the environment, the oceans, annihilating natural life

You can do nothing about it because this conduct is part of your nature

It lies in your genes

A malign cell, crouching in the darkness of your inner self, communicates to you through brain wiring

You are unpredictable

You live in a virtual dream

The virtual dream you live in makes you unpredictable

Is it your fault?

No. No for what is now past, but for what follows

It will be your fault

The Principle never finished their experiment

They left

They abandoned you

Thus, you must extract consciousness from your reason

Yet, your reason depends on the virtual reality you live in

Hence, your reason shows you a distorted reality

As a result, you do not have free will

You cannot discriminate right from wrong

ON MAN

T HE CROWD grew uneasy. The voice of Axumeriedes elevated over every thought. The captive audience bent their heads and listened.

There was never a single first Man, but many

There were no females among them

No Woman

The new creatures were not mammals

They became mammals later, centuries later, with the mutation of Woman in favor of Man

Male adults tossed into the fields

Tossed naked into life, born not yet from Woman and a Man, but from experiments made in a laboratory

There were no babies, no infants, no boys, and no adolescents among the first models of Man

The first groups of Man were monsters

Odd experimental creatures

Their brains were not yet able to perform minimal physical functions and were unable to reason

They walked supported by their four limbs

The results drove The Principle to replace one version with another

At every new version, the new creature rehearsed his first steps toward an upright position

He did so by holding to the genetic technology that gave him life

Despite how you may feel in your innermost self, you are still primitive creatures

Your life runs on virtual reality, that is the result of your internal impulses and external feedback

A blueprint of a new version of the human creatures was ready for testing when The Principle left

The map of a more completed human

A perfected creature

Perfect concerning themselves, other creatures, and the environment

It was the blueprint of what should have been the Absolute Man

The Principle departed, leaving behind their project, unfinished

Yet, you managed to survive

You managed to function, despite you being unfinished creatures

You did, you do, yet you are not doing well

You can see for yourselves that you are not doing well

You perceive that things could and should be different

Yet, you have not had the will or the tools to change the status quo that you yourselves as a race have created

You must accept that it has been hard for you

The abandonment is what I mean

Surviving is what you have been doing for thousands of years

Survivors you are, it is true

Yet, you are not free

You do not know what freedom is

Abandonment is what has been, throughout all your history as a race, your freedom

You roamed the Earth and felt free by doing it

You have felt free to explore and transform the Earth to your whims

You gave birth to gods and put words in your gods' mouths
so as they could let you do so

Until you decided on just one God

Yet, no one authorized you to do what you have done to the
Earth

You are not alone on the Earth

The Earth does not belong to you

You are not alone in the universe

You are not free to roam the universe

Eyes are watching every one of you from behind your
dreams

The restless crowd seemed to cover every angle of the
field and moved in waves as an angry sea. Voices surged
from diverse points, and their words were like an explosion
of breakers crashing against the rock that was Axumeriedes'
calm attitude and electric personality. Cries shocked the air —
more than cries, prayers.

There was a breakthrough in the experiment

The new creature stood upright and walked erect

It was a turning point in the development of Man

Once Man learned how to walk upward, Man began to think
—

And so it has been for thousands of years; humans walking

in the upright position

Walking and then thinking

Is that not what you all do, walk, and think?

And how many of you walk but only think

Walking blind, not seeing where you are going

And who of you walk the talk?

Axumeriedes walked toward the multitude, and people opened a path for him. His feet were about one inch above the ground. The crowd stirred to get a glimpse of Axumeriedes, to touch him. They were not adults, but children, as Axumeriedes had portrayed them. Incomplete adults. Abandoned creatures.

"Master!"

"Master!"

"Father!"

"Father!"

Axumeriedes calmed them with his incredible magnetism and said,

Reaching your actual unfinished version of the Homo sapiens was not linear

The new species that came to inhabit the Earth were for many years under the scrutiny of The Principle

A man from the crowd stepped in front of him and pointed at Axumeriedes.

"We're not children of a gang of extraterrestrials!" the man cried.

All ears were alert. Quickly a group of irate people, mostly men, advanced some steps closer to Axumeriedes.

"Yes, man," another man said. "Where do you leave God in your discourse?"

And then another, at Axumeriedes' back, screamed, "God is our Creator!"

And then another man, irritated, stopped in front of Axumeriedes, raised his fist in Axumeriedes' face, and exclaimed with a sharp scream, "You're the Antichrist!"

The sound of souls adrift, and then a choir of discontented voices.

And Axumerides said,

ON GOD

You will always be a religious kind, and you must be, but God will be out of this equation

Once you are back to being who you should be, God will no longer be necessary

In the minds of the multitude, figures of God were forming according to each person's beliefs and faith. And they wondered, what does he mean? Would he be talking about those miraculous apparitions of virgins or celestial entities? And, who were the chosen ones to receive advice from those Gods, and of what kind?

You believe in many things, and you think that these messages come from external sources

They are not

As I said before, they are from the Gods within

They are dormant cells that awake in any generation

Someone cried, a cry of anguish that echoed in the souls of

those gathered there, "If it is not God, then who is He who speaks?"

In the measure that touches you, It is God

It comes from within you, from your faith

From what you have learned since The Principle abandoned you

I tell you: the creation of the supernatural being you call God is a defense against the abandonment of humans

Yet, in the humans attached overlapping virtual reality, God lives in between humans' lives

You ask for God when things go wrong, and you forget Him when things go right

For you all, no matter your beliefs, your God is fear and hope

You fear that things will worsen

You hope that things will improve

And what if the God you have so many expectations about is but the Commander of an alien spaceship?

The crowd went berserk.
"You're the Antichrist!"
The fighting with the police intensified. Some religious groups clashed with anarchist groups, where others formed barricades made of burning tires. The police and media helicopters never stopped their whirling around the site. An

invisible wall separated those in chaos from those who wanted to hear the message in peace. Axumerides was oblivious to the chaos his words produced and continued his teaching,

The God you prayed to throughout each civilization was not one but many

They all might have been officers of an advanced alien exploration kind

Beware then, of their next visit

The crowd stirred.

Yet, I do refer to the God of your hopes, the God you have created to look after you, the God that justifies your actions, the One that forgives you and promises you the Heavens

It is your personal God, made to your image, measurement, and convenience

The God you carry in your mind and heart has not evolved as it should

Hence, you bring one more burden on your shoulders

The image, presence, and action you have of God has remained fixed in your mind and heart

Yet, God does not live in your heart but in your hopes

And you know now what lies within your hopes is but emptiness

Therefore, your faith holds like the roots of a tree with many branches, many leaves, and little fruit

And I ask you, this so deeply ingrained emptiness in you, is that why you need a God?

It is as if every elementary particle within yourselves claim for a lost father

If you want to adopt a God, embrace nature instead, and you would not feel empty anymore

Thus, I will tell you about God

God is nature and the force of it

God is a natural phenomenon, the sun and the moon, the rain, and the air you breathe

The thunder, the lightning, the Earth, the water, the fire, the stone, the mountain, and the tree

A blade of grass, the sky, a grain of sand, the sea, a drop of water, and the storm

God is a man and a woman, and everything in-between

It presents in the form of an animal, a bird, or in the appearance of another human being

The natural God reigns over the living creatures, and all on Earth is Its dominion

Nature is the only immortal, omnipresent, omnipotent, omniscient God

It is here for you, all over

You have always tried to deceive God

Yet, you are fooling yourselves, and you are deceiving your human nature

Humans and God are not two separate entities

One cannot live without the other

That is why the immortal, omnipresent, omnipotent, omniscient God amended this error

He divided Himself into infinite minimum parts and came to dwell in every man's and every woman's soul

God is not invisible; It is present in you for you to see It

If you seek an intimate God to love, seek within you

Love thyself

Because if you want to reach God in Its Wholeness, first you have to understand yourself in your wholeness

God is the accumulation of energy in your mind

The accumulation of love in your heart

Thus, the closer you are to yourself, the closer you are to God, and this is when you love yourself

And the closer you are to your neighbours in love and understanding, the closer you are to God

Expand God, grow with It

Push God to become the Promise you hoped for when you created Him

Make your faith universal

Do not be afraid of believing

Yet, you have created a small God, a reduced God with whom anybody can become intimate

This figure is not universal but personal

A God concerned with the little affairs of men and women

It hides in temples, travels in clouds, has a representative on Earth

You say that God created the universe, and the universe created you

And I say that you humans created your universe and held God inside it as a prisoner of the whims of humankind

You cannot represent wholeness because it is beyond you Free God from your traumas and the Heavens will open to you

Open your mind. Heaven is but an open mind

Do not use what is in you to imitate the work of God

Live within your boundaries

Do not step up to become a God

No rights have you received to rule over life, nature, will, or consciousness

Use what is in you to improve yourself, but do not ever challenge God

For though God rejoices in you, He is also wary of you

Thus, imitating God will not make you a better creature

For whichever it is, it will be but a bad imitation

The only exemption to this rule is art, but be wary of what you qualify as art

If you want to become closer to God, free from yourself, and embrace nature, then help others to move on His path

Though God lives in you, you are not in Him, and this should be your struggle

Do not seek God in temples built upon humans' profession, for God lives in humans and nature

Do not manipulate God's will with your prayer

Make your request to God honest and straightforward; never try, in the manners of humans as they do, because humans tend to become intimate with God

Most things you wish come from your internal impulses

No God can control these impulses, only you can

The crowd felt urged to pray and prayed for themselves and for the man who came from the unknown to tell them who they are and what to do to stop being who they are. And they heard their voices as their voices joined others, and the praying flowed with tears or laughter. The praying ended, and

a long silence followed, and the crowd came back to be themselves, and it was as if they all had awoken from a dream.

Do not use what is in you to imitate the work of God

Live within your boundaries

Do not step up to become a God, for you have received no
right over life, nature, will, or consciousness

Use what is in you to improve yourself, but not to challenge
God

For though God rejoices in you, in one soul, It is also wary
of you

Thus, imitating God will not make you a better creature
because whatever this imitation is, it will be a bad one.

You are still in a primitive estate, the Homo sapiens'
condition

Your reasoning is still in a primeval stage

You are so behind that you still fear, hope, speak of races,
and kill your neighbor

Fear is a cage, and you have put your God in this cage

The cage's lock opens with a key, which is hope

A lock that does not exist, and a key that does not exist, for
it is all fear

Hence, a man's heart is not a nest, but a cage

God is in you, which is true, but you are not of God, and

this is why you cannot see God face to face

You cannot see the truth

You cannot feel happiness

God, in your heart, is a prisoner of your fears because your human condition is fear

So, you should ask and pray, wish and scream, and empty your fear into the sky, which is God's mirror

And the universe will respond, and the cage will break, and you will be free because you are Gods — prisoner Gods in a cage of fear, and you know not about this

And another lonely, pungent scream.

"You are the Antichrist!"

Do not fear, people of this planet you call Earth

Fear makes you the weakest creatures on this planet

Fear within is what leads to your actions

ON THE HUMAN BODY

Life feeds from your body, and thus it has a limited time

Hence, you must keep your body strong and healthy through food and exercise

The correct food in quality and quantity, and the right exercise, in quality and quantity

Let me focus on your body for an instant

What you know about your body are but simple things

You come, grow, live, and die in it, yet it is little what you know about it

You think you do

You grow, work, love, procreate, get sick, and die

But you know little or nothing of what your body is or what is inside it, how your organs maintain the extraordinary synchronicity that keeps you alive

Can you control these processes?

Can you have access to them?

Can you alter this magnificent mechanism?

Yes, you can

You do, but you do not have the know-how to do it, yet

And you act, work, love, and think, driven by the amazing internal action that takes place inside you

You take for granted the incredible biological feat that takes place inside you

It is when you feel sick, with pain here and there that you grasp that there is something under your skin that troubles you

What you know about your body is a mystery to you all

Unless you are physicians, and even though a specialized physician

If the body works well, you do not care much

You go on with your life as usual

It is when you feel sick that there is a problem

Depending on the severity of what affects you, your interest in your body develops

But even then, you focus on the knowledge of the affected area and what produces the illness

What do you know about your body?

If you know what your skin encloses, you would see your-selves differently

If you knew more about what is under your skin, you would better understand your condition as inhabitants of this planet

It would be best to learn about the bond between your blood, organs, muscles, and bones

Once you have this established, you must know about the link between your body and the universe

Your internal organs work independently from your will

They all work in marvelous synchronicity that keeps you alive

They labour away from your thoughts; you cannot yet order them to act or react

You can give orders to some muscles to perform activities

You can shape your body externally, up to a point, you can do that

And to achieve this, muscular tuning, you have to work, and you have to work hard

You cannot because you do not know yet how to give a mental order to your muscles, or bone structure, to be different

Sometimes your internal organs get ill, and you do not know that unless you have a symptom

Yet, some illness has no symptoms at all, until when it is too late

If you do not have this sign, the sick organ will worsen

Silently, the sickness can jump onto other organs, and your entire body can fail and die

Anyhow, a warning sign brings you to see a doctor, and so on

Any physician can tell you about this

And this all happens inside your body, and yet, you know nothing about it

You do not yet know what and how things happen there, what dramas and stories develop in your body

You do not know how many heroes and villains you carry within you every second of your life, yet you know not how to control these processes

Your body is a miraculous creation

You come to life, starting by being a minute living hope in the womb of your mother

But, it is your body, and what do you know about it?

What do you know about the processes that take place every second in this astonishing box?

You do not have access to any of these "actions" that keep you alive

A doctor has them, but you, the owner of your body

You do not have command over your internal organs

If they could work at your will, it would be a fantastic achievement — a great leap forward to bring humans beyond the Homo sapiens quality

To have full control over the beating of your heart, or the circulation of your blood, or the workings of your brain, heart, kidneys, liver, pancreas, lungs, stomach, intestines, prostate, etcetera

Imagine your lives if you were able to control the automatic processes of your body

Women could control their gestational periods without the need for artificial means; they could choose when to become mothers

Men, of course, could govern their impulses

And you all could learn of better ways to keep your organs healthy

And in the case of sickness, you could be able to repair a damaged organ without external intervention

I say to you that it is possible

You are entities created with a built-in automatic repair system

Thus, it would be best if you learn how this system operates

It will help if you know how your brain works

This knowledge should be mandatory for all human beings

Educate your mind to work beyond the routine tasks you have assigned it to perform

Educate yourselves on the powerful capabilities of your

brain

You know about one of its effects: thinking limited yet enough to your needs

Push forward your knowledge of brain physiology, system, hemispheres, nerves, neurons

Learn how to activate the extraordinary feature that governs your entire body

Your brain is a universe of incredible possibilities

Make your brain the vigilante organ of your entire body

Share this cognition with every human being

A recurrent failure is that you do not share your gathered experiences with your neighbours

Do not be afraid

Alone, you cannot do what will promote you onwards to the first floor of the house

You have to do it together

Get rid of politics, jealousy, mistrust, race, religion, nations

The only nation that will survive every apocalypse is a true-knowledge nation

True-knowledge will fill the vacuum you are in now

True-knowledge is shared knowledge

Grow further away from the Homo sapiens and its traumas
It has been my discourse throughout this time here with you

Help yourself to a new dawn in human history

Be the human you should be

Learn about your body functions

The internal and the external, from the information your brain gives you

You should be able to "see" how your body performs: bones, organs, blood vessels, skin, everything because nothing in your body escapes the vigilance of the brain

You should be able to take part in every process that takes place inside your body

You must access the network of neurons

Understand every message sent and received by the brain

Every internal and external organ is subject to the brain

In a malfunction, the brain will cure the affected organ without the need for external intervention

Learn how to make your brain work to its full capability

This exercise will bring you closer to the human beyond sapiens

You can do things you never thought possible you could do

You have what you call your primary senses, which are many, many more than the basic ones you know

Your senses are tools you can use at will

These gifts will come back to you when you become the

Absolute Genus

You cannot use your senses the way you should be able to because of your status as Homo sapiens

The Homo sapiens' condition limits you, and you know about this already

The five senses you all are more familiar with are seeing touch, smell, taste, and hearing

As the Absolute Human, you will be able to perceive things through your primary five senses, but you will do so at a degree beyond what you ever imagined

You will be able to control your senses and combine them at will

You will hear a sound and see what it is that produces the sound

You will see and feel what you see as if you were touching the object with your hands

You will taste things that are miles away from you; their fragrance will come to you by your sense of smell

You will smell, see, taste, touch, and hear an object, all at the same time

Any of the senses you use will drag the others so that all sensations will come to you together

Yet, your actual status as Homo sapiens does not allow you to develop these skills

This kind of power demands education and responsibility

You will train your senses, as well

You will train them to connect with your stomach

Smell, sight, taste, hear, and touch must build a protective wall around your stomach

In your actual condition, Homo sapiens, your senses are the enemies of your stomach

Your stomach is the most abused organ in your body

You must love yourself, and this means you must love your body, your whole body: your internal organs, your blood, your skin, your bones, your brain

The whole of you

You use your stomach as a trash can

Yet your life resides in your stomach

By abusing your stomach, it is your life that you are treating poorly

All systems within your body are interconnected

Anything you chew and swallow goes to your stomach

These actions generate a unique digestive process, which you know nothing about

Changes in your diet upset your stomach

It upsets other organs that are active in the digestive process as well

Diet change is a bad habit that hinders the human body from growing healthy

You do not need much food in your stomach

Eat only to the point that you no longer feel hungry

Never fill your stomach

Your stomach is alone in the context of your body

It is defenseless

The stomach has several enemies

They are your five senses, a constant change of diet, and lousy eating habits

A voice came through the breathing of all, and it shook some.

"Are you saying that we should eat one thing, as cows do?"

And Axumeriedes responded,

Do not feed according to the voices of the industries you created

The food you eat determines your character

You may eat more than one thing, yet be careful how you mix your food

Your food must be few, and the same type and quality

Do not mix ingredients

It will be challenging, but your entire body will thank you

for this

Avoid those places where you have easy access to a variety of food

It is there that your senses betray the stomach

Feed on a few things. Less is better

Never overload your stomach

Start a pattern of alimentation and keep this pattern for years ahead, for your entire life

Your stomach, your body, and your mind will appreciate it

Eating the same food every day is a plus to your body

If there is a need for some extra proteins, minerals, or vitamins, the body itself will provide them

Your bad eating habits make your stomach, your body, and your mind suffer

Never experiment with your stomach

Do not treat it as if it is a garbage can

Be aware of artificial ingredients in the food

Many of these ingredients are either manipulated or contaminated

Even produce grown on farms are subject to contaminants

A clean, simple, steady diet is the solution to a healthy stomach, a strong body, and a sharp mind

About your skin

Your skin is the holy wrapping of all the wonders which is your body

Your skin is in itself a wonder

Do not hurt it

Do not pierce it

Do not cut it

Do not put anything strange on it

Do not abuse it

When bathing, use the appropriate temperature

Never expose your skin to too high or too low temperatures

You should always keep your skin in range with the body temperature

Love your skin; it encloses you, your life, and your God within it

Train yourself in the care of your body

Your spirit depends on it, and your immortality as well

A man was casting stones at him and hid his hand among the crowd. The crowd moved uncomfortably. The stones hit Axumeriedes and blood came from his head and face. Some men held the man and presented him to Axumeriedes. The man struggled to get free from his captors.

Axumeriedes said, like a father speaking to his son,

Are you okay? Are you hurt?

The man kept his face down.

You have hurt yourself

Axumeriedes extended his arm, touched the man's shoulder, and the man shook as if touched by an electric shock.

Axumerides said to the men who held the man,

He can go

The men released the man, and he disappeared into the multitude. People were disappointed. They expected a severe punishment from Axumeriedes, but he just let him go. Two women came. Axumeriedes sat down on the ground, and the women cleaned and bandaged his wounds. He let them do it, and the multitude waited. The women finished their work and left. Axumeriedes stood upright, and the populace cheered. One minute ago, they hated him, and now they loved him.

Axumeriedes started walking. The bandages on his head looked like a crown. People chanted behind him. The procession went on for a long time, and after a while, they reached a square. It was a plain field with some rachitic trees trying to survive the pollution emanating from the adjacent factories. The multitude occupied every possible space. Some people climbed and sat on the tree branches.

Standing on the little space left for him, Axumeriedes addressed the multitude. He signaled his bandaged head and said,

Fear is a stone you cast against yourselves

Do not hurt yourselves

Do not fear

If you are not strong enough to accept the truth and change, you will suffocate the Earth

The Earth will die, and you all will die

Again, voices of protest rose from everywhere within the crowd.
"Aw, man! The Earth has suffered threats many times before!"
"Yeah, The Earth will survive no matter what!"
And Axumeriedes said,

The Earth has survived many threats before

It will not survive the attack of more than nine billion hungry creatures

Your demographic explosion is depleting the Earth's resources at an outrageous speed

The Earth's resources are for all who inhabit it, not only for you

Land and oceans, lakes and rivers, air and forests, savannas and mountains

Every creature on this planet, save for humans, lives in balance with nature

Every natural creature lives and dies following the strict rules of its natural law

Natural law is what the human creature altered

A natural balance that the human creature upset

The Earth suffers under the dominion of artificial predators

You are the artificial predators

At this point, there was another attempt against him. Another man from the crowd threw a stone with force, but this time it was all different. Almost at one inch of reaching Axumeriedes' head, the stone made an arch like a boomerang and turned back to he who had thrown it. Yet in the face of this man, it fragmented into multi-coloured sparks. The crowd marveled.

And Axumeriedes said,

Cast stones at no one

The stone you cast against your neighbour will hit you twice

Do not wish wrong to your neighbour

You must know this already

People sought him who had cast the stone, but the man submerged into the sea of heads.

ON IMMORTALITY

S OMEONE FROM the crowd said, "Are you immortal?"
And Axumeriedes said,

What does it mean to be immortal for you?

He surveyed the crowd, now involved in profound silence.

I will tell you

Immortality is a chain formed by links of dust that humans'
anxiety forges in the anvil of time

It is a mystery that has pursued you since your creation

Imagine yourselves in one hundred years

It does not matter your age now

The important thing is to see yourself in this future scenario

If you can see yourself there, it's because you will be there

Once you are ready, breathe deeply, and hold the air as
much as you can

It is something similar to as if you were to go underwater, deep under the water, for the waters of the future are abysmal

You are a time traveler now, you, one more human being walking the sidewalks of crowded streets in the city of the future

Things will have changed, but you will be the same person

You can walk on the streets of time, but the time has not trapped you

It is because it is only your mind that travels

For what your flesh, skin, and bones cannot do, your mind does

Thus, in that corner in the city of the future, you are a free person

In this condition, you can remain there in the future

Or return to the present

You cannot return to your past

That is a myth, for there is no past, just present, only present

For past exists but in your mind

Past is but the present you skipped out on living

Thus, you can only come back to the present

But only if you happen to find it when you return

If it happens, you may not find things the way they were

when you left, and this is the trick of time: when you turn your back, even for a second, all things become different

Anyhow, you climb up a hill, and from there, you can see a road

You go to this road and stand there

The road that rolls and quickly fades away behind you is your present

The road ahead of you is your future

It is the same road; it is your life, present, and future

Suddenly, a voice reached all ears, and all eyes turned, seeking its origin as a humble human natural reaction.
"As simple as immortality to order?"

And Axumeriedes responded,

As simple as the order of immortality

In their imagination, the crowd watched the future city, and it became a labyrinth to them. Then they raised their eyes toward the sky, seeking a star to guide them, but it was not clear yet. Nothing was yet visible in the cerulean vastness. However, the light came in the shape of words on Axumeriedes' lips.

Neither is the future attached to your imagination nor is time attached to your feelings

And if you see yourself in that city of the future, do not

touch anything

Because imagination contaminates what it touches

But you, humans, do not see it this way

You see immortality differently

You want your lives to extend indefinitely; you want to be in the future as you do in the present, flesh and soul

Someone said, "Is it possible?"

I tell you that it is possible

Yet, you should be aware that as time has its tricks, life does too

Someone cried, and the question hit everybody's soul, "What then is immortality?"

And Axumeriedes responded,

I told you already. Immortality is a chain formed by links of dust that humans' anxiety forges in the anvil of time

Voices raised in unison, "But what do you mean by 'links of dust'?"

Links of dust is what you are

Links made of dust that form an infinite chain

Hence, the exercise I just introduced to you

And so, you will recognize yourself in the future, for the years are irrelevant

The numbers do not matter

What is important is your presence in those years, yet to come, your presence here and there and beyond

Then you will live forever without the need of drinking the water of the Fountain of Youth or any magic potion

Thus, any second you live your life to the fullest will make you immortal

The answer to the equation: plus heavens and minus hell, is eternal life, meaning you

Death is always within you

Death is the horizon in the landscape of your life

You should not be afraid of death, and you should not wait for it

Death, like life, is within you, always with you

One cry came from many throats, as all minds were sharing the same concern, "Is death the horizon of my life?"

Death is the horizon of your life

You live in a magical world — your virtual reality

In your reality, nothing is yours

Everything is but an illusion, everything is a mystery, a kind of world where you ask a God to come and join humanity, but nothing changes

Such a miracle! And nobody sees it, for this is the humans' world

Let it separate from the natural world, a beautiful, incredible world

However, you do not know it, and you do not see it

And you do not see the world as it is because of your ignorance, which is not life, although it is not death, either

This way, in the full enjoyment of your life, your constant inquietude is: When am I going to die?

Which is a recurrent question

This concern has accompanied you since the first spark of intelligence lit your brain

And the answer lies in front of you, in front of your eyes: on the horizon

Thus, you must open your eyes

Humanity

Human-Unity that courts eternity

What is here on the Earth is here for a reason

You know not what this reason is

You know not, but you should know it

Everything you do affects the Earth, and thus, something changes in you too, in your inner world

And something changes in the universe as well, and it is

why immortality turns against the human being

Humanity does not obey the rules of the universe, either

You, Rebel Children of the Cosmos, do not want to know where your feet stand

That is why you cannot read the signals in nature even though these are the signals that guide your path on Earth

If only you knew and followed these signals, I assure you, your passage through this life would be harmonious

You would be happier persons for you need no institutions, no machines

Neither you need to divide the Earth with borders, nor your soul into gods to live your life in full

Open your eyes and ears

It is no longer enough to walk, think, and listen

You also have to watch out, to see, and understand the signals

One of these signals is on the top of a hill, where life beats

Another of these signals is on the line of the horizon, where life ends

But why would you want to learn about the day, if not the exact date, of your demise?

In what way will this knowledge help you, or anybody else, for that matter? And if you know, would this knowledge bring something different to your life?

Wanting to know about your death is a very personal thing, yet

What I know is that if someone is going to face the truth, the best thing to do is to be ready

Hence, give yourself a moment in solitude

Stand on the summit of a hill, any hill, watching toward the horizon
It must be a natural and raised place, a lonely place, so a hill is a better place for this exercise

You must find yourself alone there

You, standing on the hilltop and the landscape in front of you in all its extension

And you and the horizon with nothing between that may hinder your sight

You may choose the time

It does not matter what time of the day it is, as the essential thing is that you have a clear view of the horizon

Once you are ready, close your eyes, and breathe deeply

Empty your mind of any thoughts you may have

Fill your heart with gratitude and do it with passion until your heart overflows with tears

Open your eyes

And you will see that the horizon line is now either closer or further away from where you are standing

The distance that exists between you and the horizon is the time you have left to live

You must prepare yourself for this exercise because it may happen that when you open your eyes, you may find that the line of the horizon is at your arm's length

Yet, you still do not exactly know how long your life is going to be

You do not know it precisely, in years, months, weeks, days, hours, minutes, seconds —

You will know this by reckoning the distance between your eyes and the line of the horizon

But what do you know about the distance?

Is it a physical, temporal, spatial distance?

You know that distance separates two geographical points or time, but that is not all

Space exists in between, and this space holds its secrets

Space is another dimension about which you know little

What will happen from this point to that point?

You measure life as if it happens within a time frame, and it is wrong

Life surges in space — a dimension

You measure death as if it happens within a time frame, and it is wrong

Death surges in space — a dimension

People are born independent of clocks and calendars

People live independent of clocks and calendars

People die independent of clocks and calendars

But no one can be born, live, and die, independent of space
 Life needs space, and death erases that space

He/she is no longer with us

It is what you say

In the exercise, I propose, the distance between you and the
horizon is your share of space still left for you

This space lies between your life and your death

Measure the distance from your feet to the line of the
horizon

You can measure this distance in any unit of space you are
familiar with, that is meters, kilometers, or miles,

yards, it doesn't matter, for space is independent of your
measurement units

The total you will divide by the time that you have lived

It could be years, months, days, even hours, minutes, and
seconds, if you happen to know this invaluable data

The distance from your eyes to the line of the horizon
divided by the time you have lived until that moment will
tell you how much time you have to live

Strong emotions shook them all, and tears fell from most eyes. A voice said, "Is this true?"
Another voice echoed, "Can we do this?"
And Axumeriedes responded,

I would rather prefer if you asked me if it is appropriate to do it

A voice raised above the others, "What then, are we not the owners of our bodies, of our life, of our destiny?"

Life and destiny are two parallels lines over which your bodies run

Life and destiny accept themselves, but they do not belong to each other

They do not form a whole

Your body connects to life and destiny and from both receives and delivers

Your body is not a point of union between life and destiny

Life and destiny run along in this parallel line of existence

Neither life feeds from destiny nor destiny feeds from life

Life and destiny go hand in hand outside the body, but they do not grow in solidarity with each other

The spirit generates life

I will talk to you about the spirit, but I will because you need to know what the spirit is

The body does not generate life, and life does not activate destiny

Like a windmill

The windmill is the human body

So as the wind moves the blades, life moves the body

The wind brings dust, aromas, and water with it, and this is destiny

And so, as the windmill does not generate the wind that turns its blades, the body does not cause the life that propels it

And what is life without a conscience but bare existence

You learn, therefore you experience

And this is what you are, but not life

Likewise, the windmill gets the wind force, so the body gets the power of life that comes from the spirit

And so, whatever action the body generates because of this effect is what you call life

Yet, there is plenty of talking about you human beings, who believe you are owners of your life and destiny

And I am telling you that you own nothing, nothing is yours, and it is all but an illusion

For even your dreams, you possess not

For even your thoughts, you own not

For authority on your tongue, you have not, for it betrays you at every instant

You do not influence your organs; most of them are independent of your will

You do not control your body, for your body may break at any moment, as happens with any fragile matter

You do not have power over the ground you step on because it may open to receive you at any instant

And you cannot say "my death" because you do not own your death, either; your death owns you

But then, if nothing belongs to you, and you still want to become immortals, at least you should claim ownership of your little moments

You should learn to live infinitely every mortal moment that life gives you

You should learn to build your passion and then live with it, not by it

For you should never become the slave of your passion

And you should never let your passion trick your destiny

For it will be like swimming with much force against the current until you are exhausted, and then the current will sweep you downstream

Enjoy every moment of your life so that every moment expands in your memories for ten, twenty, or even one hundred years

And if you will not be in that city of the future in body
and soul, as you would love to be, at least you must live a
second of your life completely satisfied

And then, you can say that you have defeated death, for
death is not a match for happiness

Keep in mind that death awaits beyond the union of the
spermatozoid and the egg and that between the fertilized
egg and death, there is a history you must take care of

For your life history will be your only and true immortality

Upon these words, the multitude remained silent for a long
time, and in the silence, Axumeriedes said,

You have your needs, I know

Go now, rest, eat, drink, and share your meal, share my
words

He began walking. Up in the sky, several media helicopters
disturbed the rhythm of the marching crowd. Axumeriedes
looked back at the mass of people that followed him.
     Voices, cries, and the multitude moved like waves in an
agitated ocean, saying, "No, don't go, Master, stay, stay!"
It has been a long session, but the people were not tired. Yet
Axumeriedes urged them to go back to their families. And so,
some of them dispersed, back to their homes and daily life,
but they all knew that there was more to learn from Axumeriedes, the interstellar pilgrim. They could follow him through
the media in his pilgrimage.

Most of them were chewing on the words of the man from the beyond. Some of them thought of the teaching they received as children. Other people were thinking about Adam and Eve and the Garden of Eden. Did this fabulous place ever exist, or was nothing real? Other people thought of God and prayed. Some of them thought of the Neanderthal man. Others of the man of Cro-Magnon, while others were thinking of the cave dwellers. And some others were ruminating on the discovery of Lucy's bones in Africa, where they say it is the place where all humans originated. And others in the crowd struggled with themselves. For it was hard for them to believe the words of that strange man whom nobody knew with certainty where he came from, albeit, they were all sure that Axumeriedes did not belong to Earth. And some thought of the advances that the human race has achieved through the centuries. And others of labs that study human genetics.

And all coincided in one thing: humans must step forward to improve the human race. Improving the human race means saving the human race and the planet. Planet Earth. All knew what the human being can do and does with nature, food, and even his kinfolk. Humans can change everything, improve anything, or destroy everything, according to their needs or ambition. Axumeriedes was walking toward a truck line, but then the light of the sunset blinded them, and they all lost sight of him.

CULTIVATE

Axumeriedes came in the morning to another city, where the people there seemed to have been waiting for him.

"Here he comes!" a child cried.

The entire city was on foot to meet him. They surrounded Axumeriedes as others had done before. The media was there too. And again, this city felt the thrill of the interstellar pilgrim's arrival. In a procession, the multitude followed Axumeriedes as they had done back in the city where he had landed. Three women came to check up on his bandage, and there was dry blood in it. They removed the dressing and marveled that the wounds had healed so fast. Axumeriedes thanked them and was ready to continue his walk when other women stopped him. They had brought water and food for him. Axumeriedes accepted the meal, sat on a bench, ate from one plate, drank water, refused more food, and resumed his walking. The multitude followed him wherever he went. A couple of neighbours offered him their balcony overlooking the plaza to address the crowd. Axumeriedes entered their house, went to the balcony, and from there, he spoke.

And Axumerides said,

Cultivate yourselves

Control the number of your population

Earth will help you if you cannot do it

The cosmos will help you if you do not want to do it

The control of your population is another opportunity for you to save your species

Transform your thoughts and behaviour because, in the next age, there will be no room for the Homo sapiens and his fanfare of ephemeral satisfactions

Understand why you must control your population

Understand why you must change your thoughts and behaviour

Speak one language

Communicate in the same language

On this small, isolated planet, you must communicate in one language

Develop a common language that refuses perversion

Use a language that enlightens the whole of you

Link this language to the vibrations of nature, the cosmos, and to your body

Create a new language that meets this condition

Learn this one language

Speak this one language

Trust your neighbour

Stop living with lies and for lies

You will not have time to build trust

You must trust blindly

Trust all humans

Educate yourselves about all of humanity and nature

As the Absolute Human, you will learn about your responsibilities as citizens of the Earth

Build the bio-society and behave accordingly

Share the Earth

Do not be afraid of sharing

You are entering into a new life

Share the welfare with all inhabitants of the Earth

Share your knowledge, all advances in science, technology, and inventions

Share the achievements you have in science and technology — be honest about your purposes

Share every discovery with the entire population of the Earth

Share all findings

Share all this with your hearts and minds open and free, in the spirit of profound humanity

Learn to leave aside jealousies, pride, politics, and other uniquely human traumas, and then, only then, you will see illuminated the first floor of this house, as you keep the basement lighted as well

Make your life easier without damaging the Earth

By sharing, you should defeat ignorance and poverty

Do not be selfish; do not be afraid of sharing

Live in harmony with yourself, your neighbours, the environment, and the cosmos

After these words, the multitude grew silent for a long time — each one involved in their thoughts. Then, Axumeriedes' voice brought them back together again.

Learn about yourselves

Learn how your mind works and how you react to the challenges that surround you

Learn how your body works

Learn about your internal and external organs and your metabolism

Analyze your behaviour when confronted with basic needs

Feel how human behaviour opposes the rules of the natural world

And again, because they were humans, the crowd stirred in uneasiness, and words flew like arrows to the heart of the stranger.

"Who are you to tell us what is right or wrong?"

"What is wrong with our behaviour?"

The way you behave among yourselves, with the environment, and with the animals is wrong

Animals, birds, insects, and spiders are the ingredients of what makes you a human being

To these words, the crowd revolved like waves in an agitated sea. Cries of rebellion were in a crescendo.

"What are you saying?"

"Aw, man!"

"You are insulting us!"

ON THE ANIMALS

Y ET, SOME people tried to appease the noisy ones, and some harsh exchanges ensued. The uproar decreased after a while. Curiosity made people pay attention to the words, and Axumeriedes continued with his message.

A new creature of a different kind roamed the landscape of the era you call the Pliocene

The first versions of the will-be-human creature that came out of The Principle's laboratory were but an inadequate being

A monster

An ugly creature with a brain too deficient to process information

A creature with the smallest ability to respond to challenges

It had a short memory and no language skills yet developed

Thus, the new creature was cold and dysfunctional

Unable to communicate, to integrate with its kind

Unable to form groups and families

The Principle eliminated them all

Then, The Principle created a second, an improved version
of this human creature

And a third, and a fourth version, and even a fifth version

Every version of these individuals began setting boundaries

The latter creature was more intelligent than the former

Imposed its presence over the other creatures, they found on
their territory

Yet, time after time, there was a call from The Principle; it
was a call to culling

A call to extermination

The first genocides took place, massive exterminations, to
improve a nascent race

It happened whenever The Principle set a new version of the
humanoid creature

Yet, some of these creatures managed to escape

And you, who are ignorant of your origins, are lucky enough
to find the bones of these first dwellers of Earth

Bones that traveled throughout the times, reaching you as a proof of their existence, to your delight, knowledge, and confusion

For it was through these culling that new and improved humans came every so often out of the laboratory's doors

The Principle updated every new version

Cerebral development, skeleton muscle, and efficient internal organs

All that came to be the essential physical part of being a human

As a result, those primeval grunts and snorts changed into onomatopoeic cacophonies

Onomatopoeic cacophonies transformed into dialects and languages

And it was on this assembly line and testing that the fanfare of acids began to get its shape

To acquire its own life

The new creature became independent of The Principle

It rebelled against its creator

Yet, to the eyes of The Principle, this individual was still deficient

The creature was nothing but a biological subconscious agent

It could hardly adapt to itself

It could hardly adapt to others

It was but a biological subconscious agent who grew alien
to himself and the environment

A voice cried out in the calmness of a multitudinous
reflection, "And how was it then that we have stopped being
biological subconscious agents?"

Axumeriedes responded,

You have not stopped being biological subconscious agents

You still are

Another uproar ensued. Frontline health workers reported
several people hurt, some with bleeding wounds. The police
could hardly control the tumult now in the hands of the violent
ones. And again, the peaceful ones tried to calm both parties,
unsuccessfully.

Someone threw a Molotov cocktail at a police car, and the
flames expanded, burning other police cars for they were all
in line to contain the multitude, and the fire reached the trees
of a nearby park. The crowd who gathered there went berserk.
Police and the army personnel were in retreat. Firefighters
struggled to put out the fire. From the spot from where he
was standing, Axumeriedes surveyed the crowd with a serene
expression, and in a moment, a magnetic current of calmness
soothed the rioters.

When it was all calm again, Axumeriedes said,

I do not condemn you for being you

Your actions measure you

All these manifestations are what you are

Yet, The Principle dreamed of another creature, a better one

The Absolute Human

And in this path to improvement, The Principle inserted in the new creature the essence of animals, birds, insects, and spiders

And again, these words woke the tumult from the somnolence that had befallen them.
"What? What is this guy talking about?"
"Silence, please!"
"Let him talk!"
"Clarify, man!"
"Explain it to us!"
Axumeriedes' voice surged stronger than ever; it filled every ear and every heart.

And Man came to life

To make the act of creation complete, The Principle took the essence of the life of animals

Diverse animals, even some already extinct, like raptors

Because all animals have a role on the Earth

The Principle mixed it with the vital essence of the life of Man

Several thousands of years later, The Principle did the same with Woman

Yet this time, in Woman, The Principle took the essence of some insects and spiders

They mixed this essence with the vital principle of every Woman

Thus, animals, birds, insects, and spiders define every human being in every aspect of their spirit, character, and body features

You, humans, have an intrinsic connection with the Earth's creatures

You have alive creatures within you

They come in you in your genes, from parents to children, to this day

Because of what is within you, what you have done to the Earth and yourselves is wrong

In your ignorance, you use animals, birds, and insects to satiate your hunger, for work, transport, for industrial purposes

You use them in laboratories for unaccountable purposes

Animals fill zoos, aviaries, aquariums

The natural world entertains irresponsible humans

You kill animals for your entertainment

You have used them. Still, you do, for experiments of any kind

You keep them as pets, helpers, companions, or guardians, in sports, gambling, rituals, and so on

It is wrong to share a roof with animals

You know what you have done

Still, you do. You persist

All this you have done and continue to do

What you have done to animals and you continue doing will cost you your privilege to live on Earth

You have disrespected nature

Contempt is what you show for the creatures that have shared their shelter with you

And despite your flaws, you think high of yourselves

You feel superior to all other living creatures

You are not

You are one more inhabitant of this planet, but you feel superior to the creatures that surround you — an expression of human vanity, a fallacy that is so easy to challenge

Dare you go naked walking in the coolness of a winter forest surrounded by hungry wolves

Dare you to stay naked in the solitude of a mountain

Dare you swim in deep, agitated waters

Do it, and you will see how long your feeling of superiority lasts

Look around you

Any natural function you perform, animals, birds, insects, and spiders also perform, and they do it even better than you do

Indeed, some species have ample advantage over humans in these tasks, and these species know no other God but nature

A cry flowed from the heart of the multitude, "You are wrong, man. God made us superior to all creatures on the Earth!"
And Axumerides responded,

A man wanted to test his superiority over the creatures of the forest

And so, he went naked into the wilderness

The man found a wolf, and the wolf came closer, smelled the naked man, and left

The man felt ecstatic with the experience

The wolf knows who I am, the man said to himself, I'm his master

The wolf came back

"Come here, wolf, the man said, I'm your master, and you, a

subject of my kingdom."

The wolf approached and crushed the man's throat with his jaws

"There!" The wolf said, " If you had mastered yourself first, then you would have built thy kingdom, but away from here, and without the pain."

I ask you all to reflect on the Wolf's words

Animals, any living creature on Earth, for that matter, are not inferior living creatures

They surpass humans in exercises of adaptation and survival. Most of them have developed within senses that would have made humans the most fantastic creatures on Earth if these were to be applied to humans. Indeed, as extraordinary as you are, you are still dysfunctional.

All living creatures are your fellows in this adventure of life on Earth

They are different, but they are your fellows, nonetheless

With them, you share the Earth. Thus, you owe them respect

You owe even more to them

While all other living creatures on Earth are givers, you humans are takers

Animals focus on living. Humans focus on having

You occupied their world, the exterior world, which is Nature, which belongs to them

And you share with them your inner world, which is the world that belongs to you

You have two worlds that should work in harmony

The Principle wanted to preserve the equilibrium between foreign and proper

Foreign meaning humans, proper meaning nature

You are the alien creatures

You are mirrors that reflect the light and the shadow, which is what you know and what is the unknown

It is what humanity is, light, and shadow

The inner animals that live in every human being balance both worlds

Once again, the crowd stirred in uneasiness as if Axumeriedes had offended them. A long pause followed. There was a tense calm. Everybody seemed to mull over the words of the man from deep space. Fires were still burning. Beyond the sea of heads, there was a fragile truce between rioters and police.
Axumeriedes surveyed the crowd, and thus he spoke,

Male humans have the essence of animals in every one of you

Female humans have the essence of insects and spiders

The Principle thought this to be not only necessary but also a must-do task

The crowd continued its restless stirring. Someone from the

heart of the assemblage cried aloud, "Why was it necessary?"

The Principle could not avoid it

They had already reached this conclusion

They had done their homework, had studied the conditions under which the human-to-be creature would survive

Corrections took place, new calculations, new studies, and new experiments

Without these adjustments, the penultimate creature would have never survived

It would have never been able to introduce exercises of adaptation. which later on allowed it to emerge forward, distinct from the other beings whose roots are in nature

Cries surged from some throats in the constant whirling of the crowd.
"What was missing then?"

Emotions, emotions were missing because what makes you a human being is not the bone structure

It is not the skeleton, or your internal organs, or the brain, or the ability to decode the senses

What makes you a human being are the emotions

Love and pain, hate and passion, conflicts and suffering, friendship and compassion, fear, and rebelliousness, and all other sentiments that flow through your heart

Emotions are what make humans react

Without feelings, any interaction among humans would be a negation of the self

It would be a negation of their neighbour's existence

So, without emotions, there would never be couples, families, communities

Without feelings, there would never be a link, a bridge between one person and the other

Yet, the emotions that allow you to subsist on the Earth will hinder any attempt you will make to survive in space

"And the animals provided us with these gifts?"

It was more of a thought than a question as if someone had interpreted the general view and expressed it aloud.

Yes, the animals, aquatic creatures, birds, insects, and spiders use their natural abilities to survive

They learn from the lessons that the water, the air, and the earth give them, and they adapt to these elements

They read nature because they are a part of it

You who inhabit this planet you call Earth, you cannot read nature

Because you are not part of nature

"Whoa! Woah there, man!"
"God made us!"

"We are nature's essential particle!"

Axumeriedes' voice raised over all other voices, sound, or noise.

Human beings are not nature's essential particle

Accept the four fundamental principles that sustain your reality:

1. Accept that humans are a foreign artificial conscienceless creature, built as a bio-techno-scientific experiment

2. Accept that humans are not — never have been— nature's essential particle

3. Accept that the Homo sapiens failed to understand the laws that govern its kind, nature, and the cosmos

4. Accept your responsibilities as a foreign species to the Earth

The acceptance of your responsibilities, not the rights you earn, will make your life liveable

Life finds its purpose, always

Do not evade your responsibilities; make your life purposeful

Remember that you are here because of the values The Principle inserted in you

The Principle understood that humans would need values

Yet, the builders made mistakes

What animal, fish, or bird looks to the sky for answers?

Just you, humans

The Principle did not foresee this error

Still, they gave you values

The source of these values are the creatures of the natural world

Without your inner animals, birds, insects, and spiders, you human beings would be but a frame with a human form

A brain without character, without passion or, will, without feelings or energy

Without the creatures of nature, you would be but an abandoned project lost in the absolute void

Even though you, the human creature, never connected with the environment

Indeed, you still are foreigners to what surrounds you

You are still strangers to the water, the earth, the fire, and the air

Questions came from one shore to the other from the sea of heads.
   "But the animals, the insects — "
"Who put them on Earth?"
   "Where did animals come from?"
   And Axumeriedes responded,

They do belong to the Earth

They are the result of evolution, yet using your own words, I say that they are the real children of God

Look into the construction of your human body. It is full of flaws.

A forced copy from the animal's species, your human bone structure is not correctly done. The Principle could not improve it because they left when you were yet in a state of experimentation

Your body design is no masterpiece

Your bone structure makes you suffer

Hurt Woman during pregnancy, hurt the baby in her womb

Hurt her giving birth

Your spine hurt you, all your bones hurt

Your internal organs are still adjusting, deciding

Your brain needs space and time to grow to expand

Space, yet it is wasted space, and vacuum fills in

Time, yet it is wasted time, and illnesses take over

You are perfect only in drawings, in art, in the hope of being perfect, the perfect being

Running away from evolution in pursuit of perfection

Forget perfection. Seek evolution within

Perfection only exists in drawings, in art, in the hope of being perfect, the perfect being

And in nature, which you ignore

You, in your human complexity, own qualities that isolate you from the environment

Yet, although nature accepted you, you do not belong to the Earth

You never will

Nature accepted you, but you were never welcome

What do you know about humankind, versus what do you know about the environment?

Your ignorance is why you do not hesitate to act against all laws of nature and your kind

You do so as soon as you learn that your God is taking a nap

As soon as you know that the police rest

As soon as you learn that the law is weak, corrupt, and deficient

As soon as you sense that some social circumstance frees you from your responsibility

Henceforth, you respond with destructive ignorance

With the wrath of daring, with the danger laziness conveys

When you feel sick, either with depression, solitude, or anguish, something in your animal part is hurting you

Thus, you should treat it like what it is: a wounded animal

But you do not know that what you have in you is a wounded animal, and thus you do not seek a cure for it because if you knew, you could heal your internal animal and would be ashamed of the way you treat the external creatures

You should never forget that you all have within a part of animal essence

Yet, in this construction involving nature, The Principle faced a paradox, which is the food chain, a natural condition in nature

Yet, animals, fish, birds, insects, and spiders they all live in a convivial atmosphere, in agreement within human's innermost nature

Within every one of you, lambs and wolves live in harmony

Bees and spiders live in peace

No insect, no spider that lives inside your body, feeds from one or the other, and this is because there is a law that keeps them in balance

Because of this law, they all feel satiated; they do not need to hunt

If this law did not exist, a slaughter would take place inside you, and there would never be a human being able to reach adult age

Axumeriedes felt the stillness of the multitude. The meek

silence encouraged him to continue.

The Principle made several modifications to the genetic
network applied in humans

Yet, a gene programmed to control the impulses evaded
depuration and mutated

It made its way through generations, and it is latent in every
one of you

This defective gene may remain dormant for the entire life
of the individual or can wake up at any moment

If it does, it activates the primordial urges every human
carries within, and in turn, triggers undesirable neuronal
activities that may become uncontrollable for the individual
and its neighbours

Two primordial urges, which prove you are artificial creatures, are crime and invention

Among the latter, which may become the former, is the
invention of weapons

Another is your craving for providing machines with artificial intelligence

Yet, the significant risk in this venture comes from the
ungovernable intelligence of the genes

Genes can operate on their own; they can be independent,
thus ignoring the network

Of course, humans are moving beyond this obstacle and

pushing paradigms further

You are on your way to creating artificial neuronal networks

On this, you cannot control the impulse to replicate the work of The Principle, your makers

I advise you not to continue

Instead, you could use this knowledge to improve your kind

You have been wrong many times already

Do not build machines

Do not provide machines with artificial intelligence

At a given moment, you will not be able to control this inventory

Do not invent objects that create mistrust amongst yourselves

They will bring forward your collective ruin

The crowd once again stirred and felt uncomfortable.

Through your inner animals, you must learn the most you can about you

These animals reflect who you are as you reflect on what they are

Thus, happiness is but a meeting face to face with the animal you carry within

Keep your inner animals alive and in harmony

The degree of harmony in this relationship will determine your degree of satisfaction

Your satisfaction should show in your face

But what I see in your face is but the leftovers of your day

It should not be that way

Think nature, live nature, respect nature

Natural beings live inside you

Live as if the mountains are your bones

Live as if the forests are your hair

Live as if the rivers, lakes, and oceans are your blood

Live as if the Arctic and the Antarctic poles and the glaciers are your teeth

As if the earth and the air that covers it all are your skin

Experience in you, the spirituality of nature, in your body, blood, organs, bones, and skin

Axumeriedes finished his message. His words kept floating in the air for a while as he disappeared into thin air as a common magic trick. The multitude moved in a to-and-fro motion as palm trees on a beach do when driven by changing winds.

ON WOMAN

THEY ALL waited until late at night for the return of the mysterious Axumeriedes, but the interstellar pilgrim did not come back until dawn. By then, many groups and families had gone back to their homes, but a significant number remained in the surroundings, watched by the police and soldiers who patrolled the city's fields and streets, arousing the radicals' wrath. There was no peace throughout the night. Most of the TV channels and other media remained there, broadcasting reviews about the event worldwide.

Axumeriedes came back at the same site, and everyone become alert to his words. He studied every person who gathered there, summoned by his presence. Every anxious face. Every open eye. Even though it was very early in the morning, the crowd grew larger by the minute. There were at least sixty thousand people.

Sixty thousand pairs of eyes followed Axumeriedes when he suddenly started walking in a straight line upon a point located at a distance in front of him. Again, the crowd opened

a path for him. Some of the people dared to touch him, patting
him on his shoulders and his back. Axumeriedes walked,
oblivious to this manifestation from the crowd. In his path,
there was a dusty field. It was then that people noticed that at
his steps, he left no tracks on the dust. Although he strode with
a normal gait, he kept his feet above the ground by about one
inch. People thought that this trait could have been another
of his miracles. In the monk's clothing, the stranger looked
even more distant. A strange sensation. Remote in time and
space from those who stretched their hands to touch him. He
acknowledged them all, though by nodding, but not smiling.
He reached his destination. An older woman was sitting there
on her walker. In her hands, she carried a bouquet.

"I have brought these flowers for you, Messenger of God,"
the old woman said.

Axumeriedes received the flowers and caressed the woman's
gray hair. The crowd cheered.

And thus it came to everybody's mind that in less than a
second, Axumeriedes noticed her, one among the thousands
in the restless multitude, knew who the woman was, where
she was, and how frustrated she felt with her age and her lack
of mobility. Having located that woman's heart in that sea of
souls was, to the spectators, another of many miracles. When
the crowd learned about the incident, they shuddered in awe.
It could have been Axumeriedes' fifth miracle, although, to
some people, this act was not a miracle at all because they
tended to weigh the unexpected with the expected as if

the impossible was a constant in their lives. And when the unthinkable happens, they don't believe it happens. This thought holds people behind throughout their lives. Then they complain because a miracle never occurs to them, and it should not be because a miracle is but the communion between faith and an open heart.

Axumeriedes kissed the older woman as a son would have done to his mother, turned around with the bouquet in his arms, and said,

Woman was a separate experiment, a different creation

The Principle did not teach you civilization, did not teach you how to live

Woman did

Woman tamed the land, learned how to work it, sow, and reap the Earth's fruits

Woman did it all, driven by her innate ability to observe the changes in nature

The sequence The Principle had followed in the making of Man did not repeat in the making of Woman

The Principle had advanced on their quest to create another artificial being

This time, their goal was to create a being that could assimilate to the Earth better than Man

The Principle built Man and Woman as different species

Man and Woman lived on the Earth separated by time and geography

The Principle created Woman thousands of years after Man, and then ended the experiment, dismantled the laboratories, and left the Earth

They abandoned their creation, leaving them without rules, and so Man wandered through, in dispersed groups, nomads clashing each time they met, disputing about land, and hunting territories, the strongest always imposing their will over the weak ones

Woman instead gathered together, organized, and established themselves in their assigned geography

Man, in their wandering, met Woman

It was inevitable

In the beginning, Woman could not bear the children of Man

She adapted her body to the seed of Man

Through the centuries, mutated her bone structure and internal and external organs

In this way, she procreated, formed families and nations, and populated the Earth

In the making of Man, The Principle implanted the essence of animals, and thus in every man's aura, you can see a wolf, a fox, a bear, a raptor, a lion, a frog, a mouse, a monkey, a lamb, and many other animals

In the making of Woman, The Principle implanted the essence of insects and spiders, and thus in every woman's aura, you can feel something of the bee and the spider, the praying mantis and the ant, the butterfly, and the wasp

The reason why men and women are so different lies in the composition of their inner world

If there is an animal similarity between Woman and Man, it is because of mutation

A mutation that The Principle overlooked at the moment of Creation

A forced mutation from Woman to adapt to Man's will

With the bear's muscular mass, the cunningness of the fox, the bull's strength, or the lion, with the brutality of a raptor, Man has trapped the praying mantis, stepped on the spider, used the bee, held the butterfly by her wings

This Man has done since his first encounter with Woman

To keep Woman under his dominion

To strip her of her magic

Albeit, Woman's inner insects and spiders help Woman to reach capricious standards

For every bull-man, fox-man, or wolf-man knows well how difficult it is for him to trap a wasp that buzzes around his head

Or how curious these same animals are with the dainty butterfly that flutters in front of their eyes

Or what can the animal do if a bee pierces the bear's
heart or if the wolf's brain entangles in a spider's web of
emotions?

To trap the soul of a Woman, or even to know her feelings,
is a difficult task for Man

And as a shield, Woman uses the camouflage of the praying
mantis

And like a bee, an ant, or a butterfly, Woman has always
been busy taking care of herself and others

She keeps herself full of activity: maintaining her appearance, arranging the home, getting pregnant and giving birth,
taking care of her husband and children, organizing the
domestic expenses, taking care of the gardens and greenery,
preparing food, nursing the wounded, plus a thousand other
tasks

As a reward, she retires, mute and anonymous, to rest
eternally at the shadow of the gravestone of he who was her
husband

Man often talks about the Woman's cry, but never about the
Woman's silence

Woman's silence is more deafening than any cry

Yet, Man has no ears for the silence of Woman

Since the beginning of their association, Woman has lived
in the shadows of Man

And from that shadow, she has claimed her independence,

an individuality that Man has never understood

Someone from the crowd asked, "Why did The Principle create males and females at different times, and so far away, geographically, from each other?"

And Axumeriedes answered,

The Principle did not create males and females

Gender in humans is a condition, a reaction, a mutation, a by-product

Sex in humans is a subject of expression

In nature, sex is a tool for the survival of the species

The Principle's concern was about neither sex nor reproduction

Sex for pleasure and reproduction is a distortion that came through the idea of freedom

Yet, despite all the advances you as humanity claim, sex still is a wall that separates you

You must think beyond what divides you

With the making of Woman, The Principle wanted to experiment again, yet with Woman, there was a different start

By then, The Principle had a different vision of what they proposed when they conceived Man

They wanted a being who linked other elements from nature

They wanted a complete being and not only that but a creature more in tune with nature

The Principle knew that Man would never be a creature in tune with nature because of the way that Man was developing

Sooner or later, Man would grow away from his source of life

Woman would have been the creature that governed the Earth

It did not happen because The Principle departed, abandoning their work

Left to themselves, Woman developed differently than Man

They did not go hunting, nor did they fight in wars

They remained in their place; they studied nature and adapted to it, which Man never did

Woman never sought weapons, but tools instead, tools to work the land and build shelters

Woman reproduced, yet without the seed of males

Woman's offspring were only females

Through parthenogenesis, Woman could develop her eggs without fertilization

They could do it, yet Woman lost this form of asexual reproduction when she had to mutate her body to receive Man's seed

At the beginning of times, Man wandered, hunted, dreamed, and made wars

In another region, in another continent, Woman collected the fruits of the Earth, learned from the cycles of nature, and built shelters for them and their all-female progeny

The Principle's purpose was not to populate the Earth

They did not make humans as male/female with the idea of populating the Earth

Man and Woman were two different projects

They grew separately as diverse entities in their respective pre-assigned geographical regions

This status quo ended when both species met

Man, being the more aggressive and muscular of the two, became the dominant one

And then, over thousands of years, Woman mutated to accept into her body the seed of Man

It was not an easy task

She had to change her bone structure in a way to conciliate with her standing erect and balanced while keeping her shape, size, and weight, while carrying in the narrow space inside her, one or several voracious alien creatures with a compressed brain, which decompressed at birth and continued expanding throughout the years of their life

Axumeriedes made a long pause. The crowd mulled over his words. All was quiet now as if they were themselves suspended between worlds. People were thinking about the crash of worlds. The collision between both species must have been brutal. They all had the same thought. The planet of water was restless. And they imagined how the scenario of that first encounter between Man and Woman could have been. They fancied a valley, a river crossing through under the shadows of snowy peaks. They imagined female communities gathering at the bonfires. The children, all girls, roaming freely around. Were they alert, these women? Why? They should not have been. They had no enemies. For thousands of years, they had grown unmolested there in their territory. Which territory was it? Was it Africa? Was it Asia?

The beasts were not a threat to them, as Woman was not a threat to the animals. They had dwellings already, for they were never nomads. Man was. Woman built their houses from the materials they obtained from nature. Same as their food, they did not dwell in caves. They had already learned to tame the soil so it could yield produce. They had discovered how to sow and harvest and store for the cold days. And they did not kill animals for consumption, for they were not carnivores. Their metabolism has not yet mutated to process the proteins found in meat, which came later with their union to Man.

Woman made their clothes. They knitted the fruits of nature, which they domesticated with the help of The Principle. Woman learned from the bees, ants, butterflies, praying mantises, spiders, and wasps. And they knew about flowers, threads, woven, fabrics, and colours.

Were they pretty? Those women, the primitive ones, were they good-looking? Axumeriedes read the crowd's thoughts and would have explained to the public that beauty is but a human concern, a human conceit, but opted to remain silent. Yet, the populace wanted to know.

And also, were they free in their world of women? The crowd was trying to envision the Earth of three hundred thousand years ago. Women living in peace, until one morning, these hairy monsters came down the mountains, through the jungles or desert that bordered their female kingdom. Men, exhibiting their bestiality. They were beating themselves on their chests, their penises dangling between their legs, hitting their torsos with their fists, pounding the dust with their long-nailed feet. And howling, growling, grunting, and jumping from here to there, terrifying Woman to death. And Woman had never seen such a beast before. Alas!

Nothing, absolutely nothing, could have prepared them for what followed. It was a brutal encounter. Man's ferocity set the pattern Man would follow throughout humanity's history and to this day. Ambushing, attacking, conquering, pillaging, raping, killing, destroying, and abandoning the place, carrying among their treasures the slave-woman who must follow him wherever he goes, to serve him, to bear his children, to submit to his whims, to accept it all because he is her master, her protector, her benefactor. In sum, Man is her Lord. And after thousands of years of this forced union, the Earth is still a male-dominated world. The integration of both species is but apparent. It is not real.

Axumeriedes' voice brought the crowd back from their contemplation. And as if he was reading the thoughts of each one at the same time, he said,

The differences that still separate both sexes are remarkable

I can see it in all your images, those that you have here on Earth, and those that you sent to the interstellar space

Man should have proposed a different path for Woman

A path based on the characteristics of Woman

A path that would have taken humanity to higher levels

Instead, Man condemned Woman to immanence, as dependent on Man's will

And to add salt to the wound, ancient records, claimed as divine, sealed Woman's destiny, even to this day

A question reached the front, dragged forward by the echo of thousands of throats, "What key quality makes women better than men?"

Generosity

From her condition of immanence, she offers her body so that Man can enjoy transcendence

Yet, Woman's generosity has never been enough for Man

Man always asked for more, not only from Woman but also

from the entire Earth

Throughout the centuries, Woman adapted herself to please the whims of their male partners

For, I say to you, in freedom, away from Man, Woman would have been a different being

Woman's interests differ from those of Man

If Woman had ruled, the Earth would have been an equal, peaceful, respectful world of families; No conquests, no invasions, no borders, not a single war would have ever separated families

Man alienated Woman subordinated her

Woman's nature has subordinated her as well

This condition was not in the plans of The Principle

The Principle was stranger to this superior-subordinate scale, genders, or ranking

A situation that resulted from the chance meeting of Man and Woman was a human thing

An accidental encounter

The Principle did not foresee how the creature would react once left abandoned to its means

Do not make the same mistake by instilling human-AI into machines

The Principle gave life to you, yet it denied you consciousness

Consciousness is not a right you can claim, but a privilege

You must earn it

Consciousness is a step up in the spiral to completion

It will bring you closer to being a complete individual, yet you are not

Woman has been the victim of this tragedy

The Principle planned to improve in Woman the wrongness they made in the construction of Man

Yet, they left without bringing the experiment to term

You do not have control over your internal organs

You cannot connect with the natural world

These disadvantages discriminate against Woman more than Man, for she is the one that gives birth

Most mammals gestate when they sense that there will be enough food for the mother and the creature

Their offspring limits to a few, even though many die earlier as per natural selection

Yet, Woman is immune to the signals of nature

She is at a disadvantage with other female mammals on Earth

Regardless of the difficulties around her during her ovulation period, Woman gets pregnant anyway, and she can get pregnant anytime following when her first period announces to her that she is ready for motherhood

Thus she can go on giving birth every year of her reproductive life because the egg has no mercy with Woman

The egg is within her, ready to give life, regardless of her will

The egg is behind the pleasure, the obligation, and the violence

Woman gives life, an undesired life, an inconvenient life, an untimely life, or a welcome life, it does not matter

Thus, menstruation and pregnancy are by-products of her body

These processes exhaust her, limit her, and distract her from accomplishing other tasks that she finds essential for her in her life

These changes are mutations her body went through for thousands of years

Their bodies had to accommodate to the invasive seed of Man, and these processes tired her and hindered what she may have wanted to do in her lifetime

She seeks self-realization as well

Woman must know that her task is worth it

Giving life, nurturing, and raising a family may not be enough, for she wants her labour to be transcendent, and she cannot do it, for it is Man who deprives her of this right

At the Absolute Human stage, Woman's status will change

Humans will no longer be fragile creatures

They will complete themselves in mind and body, and this change will reflect in their thoughts and spirits

Human thought will be one, and thus Man and Woman will be one

Life will have a value, and thus in the post Homo sapiens society, Man and Woman will recover their roles as assigned by The Principle

Does anything remain of your creators in your mind, in you, the modern Homo sapiens?

Yes

There are fading teachings from your ancestors

Fading instructions based on fading memories that long ago turned into religions, myths, and superstitious beliefs, which you still carry in your minds and hearts

You are artificial creatures

Do not build machines and do not provide them with artificial intelligence

Do you feel free to make your own decisions? Yes, you do. You feel free

Yet you are not free

Freedom demands moral responsibility that your actual level of consciousness cannot sustain

Free will is what you dream you have, but you do not have

There is not enough consciousness in human beings to support free will

These words signaled the end of his discourse for the day. Axumeriedes walked through the multitude. As always happened, they opened a path for him, and all wanted to touch the interstellar prophet, as some people had already named him. And because no one could match the speed of his steps, he soon left everyone behind and disappeared on the road to the river.

ON THE ALPHA WITHIN

THE NEXT day, he returned to the esplanade in the first city where he had landed in the lake. And the city had not changed, for the chaos had been permanent, for although Axumeriedes spoke in the neighbouring towns, they all followed him through the media. The multitude wavered like a disoriented herd of multi-coloured elephants. They had been rotating their place with family and friends who brought them food and water, and in turns, they took breaks to go to the portable washroom that the authorities had placed around the esplanade. Axumeriedes showed signs of neither exhaustion, nor hunger, nor thirst, even though he had eaten and drunk very little during the days he had been speaking. Axumeriedes had for sure rested and eaten. It was what people guessed he did when he was absent. Because he looked always rested and well-fed, and his voice was the same, energetic, commanding, and clear, as when he came out from the lake holding that fish and spoke to them for the first time.

And Axumeriedes said,

Man, learn about the alpha animal that lives in your body

Woman, keep your internal creatures in harmony

Man must learn about the alpha animal that sometimes, but not always, directs the herd

They are animals, and as such, they are fretful, restless, unpredictable, and wild

Be aware of these traits, for your problems begin when they wander free through every cell of your body

The alpha animal shows in your character and physique

Within you lives either a monkey, a wolf, a fox, or a lion

A bull, a bear, a pig, a cat, a frog, a sheep, or a lamb, etcetera

And you may as well identify, in the face of your neighbour, the cold eyes of an aquatic animal

Or in his attitude with regards to a given stimulus, the primitive response of a reptilian

And this applies to your behaviour as well

If your alpha animal is nocturnal, then you will never be happy in daytime activity, and vice versa

And so on in every activity you perform, you must be aware of your dominant internal animal

It does not pay to ignore it, least of all to isolate it

You know little about your origins

You consider yourselves made in the likeness of a divine entity

Yet in the whole of your actions and needs, you act as any beast would act in similar circumstances, no more and no less

You envy some natural creatures for their many qualities that you as humans do not have

For example, the beauty of an individual species, courage of others, boldness in others, their extraordinary abilities, their grace, etcetera

You envy some animals in the wild

You fear them, yet their actions are their natural response to the challenges of nature

In all these things, you humans are at a disadvantage

Even in simple things such as locating the nest, finding food, identifying who is a friend and who is the foe

The animals recognize their offspring

Humans do not recognize their offspring

The crowd began a noisy protest again. With a gesture, Axumeriedes soothed them. He covered the entire multitude with his calmness, and then he continued speaking.

And Axumerides said,

You, the Homo sapiens, forget these elementary actions

In your ignorance, you end up as prisoners in the four walls of your depression

Sometimes, the human brain disconnects from the internal animals

This action affects your internal balance

Organs, bones, and the brain suffer, and hence you lose yourselves in the labyrinths of your innermost universe

In these cases, your internal animals suffer too

And they do because they feel you have abandoned them

Therefore, your internal animals react and behave savagely

They assault the body and cause it to perform shameful actions, and then you perform heinous acts that hurt yourself and those who surround you as well

Henceforth, it is a good measure to go through life while keeping the peace and staying in touch with external nature

Make frequent visits to a park, the mountains, the country-side, and be in contact with natural water, for these actions will keep your internal animals, insects, and spiders content and in harmony

It is all that your heart needs to keep beating

And when I say 'go out and enjoy nature,' I mean enjoying it as it is without affecting it, without hurting it, and without destroying it, for any human sample left behind, any kind of garbage will show that humans have been there

Keep in mind that nature is fragile

Do not damage nature

Do not cut a tree to build a building

It's wrong, you must understand it

Killing one creature on Earth is a crime, but a human's under-developed mind and overdeveloped ego cannot, and will never, grasp the notion of that offense

Nature is one and remembers

Nature has a memory

You are the foreign creature with a brain big enough to create insanities

You who practice hunting as a sport, when it is a crime

You who support the business of weaponry to aid in this human atrocity

Atrocities

Capturing, commercializing, and domesticating animals

Exotic pets you call these victims of your ignorance

Training animals to attack humans and other animals

Invading the animals' spaces with your dwellings and presence

Such atrocities would shame any other species, except

humans, of course

Meanwhile, your inner animals feel how you destroy the world from where once upon a time they came

You are foreign creatures from whom the external animals prefer to keep a distance

Yet, the external animals can recognize the animal that lives in your body

Thus, the animal in front of you may react in different ways, and it may be cautious, curious, aggressive, or sullen, and it all depends on the kind of animal they see in you

That neighbour's dog always barks when it is near you, and you do not know why it growls at you

The dog may not see you as a person, a human being, but instead, what the dog sees is a bear, a monkey, or a raptor, and so the dog reacts in agreement to its instinct

Then that dog will attack you, despite that animal having been trained not to do so

And the dog will attack even if the person in front of him is his dearest master

And this happens all the time because you, in your naïveté as human beings, attach social values to animals

You are wrong because animals see humans as what you are, a foreign species

Worse even, given certain situations, most people believe that the animal loves them

Some episodes support this human experience, yet this view represents entirely another mistake in how humans see animals

Therefore, you must keep a distance from the external beasts and keep a distance from your domestic kind as well

These creatures must live their lives, not yours, for this is what your inner companions have done

They have abandoned their lives to live your inner life. And yet, this is another contradiction in the raising of the human being

Humans have tortured, domesticated, killed, ate, and exterminated the external beasts through the ages

They have done this either because of need, pleasure, or boredom

In doing this, humans have ignored their inner animals

Yet, animals have had and will continue having their revenge

Diverse illnesses have plagued humanity throughout the ages, and most of them come from animals

It is undeniable that pestilences that cost millions of lives have had — still have — their origins in animals

You must re-educate yourselves, to relearn to respect the animals with whom you share the Earth

All animals on the Earth

Reflect upon my words

What are animals to you?

What are you to them?

An intense silence followed. The crowd meditated upon these questions. The first question was easy to answer. Everyone knew the value that each person gives to one's pets. On other animals, the general feeling was partial or total indifference. What are you to them? The answer to this question demanded to state a sentiment but from the animals' point of view. And so, images of animals came into everybody's mind. People thought about those animals whom humans make suffer, and this happens daily in places where they have animals for experiments. People thought of the animals, birds, and aquatic creatures daily exterminated by humans. The scenes continued passing before their eyes — passages of human viciousness and brutal ignorance. People wondered if the animals could feel like humans. If humans could feel like animals do, how different would the relationship with the animals be?

A mute question was showing in the eyes of the multitude, "What should we do?"

Axumeriedes read this question, and thus he answered,

Free the external animals

Free them all

Return them to their natural world

Let all external animals roam free

Free those animals that can go back to the wild

Protect those that because of you will not survive in the wild

Free all animals

Stop this madness of using what you call intelligence to chase them, exterminate them, or have them as prisoners to soothe your loneliness

Release them all, cages and leashes no more

What is the pleasure you have in enjoying the company of a caged animal or the one you hold on a leash?

You are the ones who praise yourselves for providing your pets with all the comforts

You must show your true love for the animals by living away from them

While in your cities, the pet stores flourish, and the numbers of abandoned animals grow

While humans expand their land, the animals reduce their habitat

What you must kill is your anxiety to hunt and to exterminate animals

Stop your futuristic dreams

No zoo will exhibit the first generic animals with no relation to a natural environment

No zoo will exhibit technologically assembled beasts

It should not happen because wildlife has no replacement

Learn how to live on the Earth, if and only if you want to continue living on this planet

Learn how to live and share before it is too late for you and the Earth

His words reached every ear.

Keep a continent of animals and birds, an ocean for marine life

The crowd exclaimed in unison: "What?"

You heard me, people of this planet you call Earth, you heard me right

Keep a continent for animals and birds, and an ocean for marine life

Animals will adapt to their new home faster than they have adapted to your obsessive passion for hunting them down

Keep a continent as a park where no human being would ever have access, a place where flora and fauna can live apart from humans; no more tamed nature

It would be a different kind of Noah's ark

I would add an ocean for marine life, an ocean free from man's presence, waters free of devices made by humans

Make a part of the Earth a 'No Humans Zone.'

No more human's waste, garbage, plastic, oil spills, or any of this human activity

And all along with the land and sea, a piece of the sky too, of course

A "No Fly Zone"

A "No Navigation Zone."

Give back to the birds their sky

Give back to the butterflies and bees their natural gardens

Give them back at least a piece of sky with nothing human in it that may confuse birds and disturb butterflies and bees

It is a must, it is necessary, it is justice

You, human people, can do many things. Why then cannot you do what you should?

Why can you not do the correct thing for once?

You have taken your space on Earth by stealing it from the animals

Let justice prevail and return to them what belongs to them: life, nature, and freedom

Get far away from the external animals!

Get closer, much closer to your internal animals!

Wake up and mature

Grow to know and respect the animals that live in you

You must learn as much as you can about the nature of the animals inside you

In particular, the dominant animal in your body: you must know about their customs, way of life, habits, and etcetera

The dominant animal may become a challenge to discover

In most cases, this alpha animal lives dormant in you, hidden in someplace within your inner self without you ever being aware of its presence

It is your task to bring it to light and train it

In its identification and knowledge roots the secret of your whole life

Look at the cities the Homo sapiens have built

They have nothing to do with humanity, as you feel it

You do not build cities as cities are supposed to be for you who inhabit them

Cities must deliver satisfaction to the human being

Urbanists must consider the biological factor, the alpha factor

The leading inner animal must be present when urbanists design a city

For the atmosphere of every dwelling, of every city, must replicate the nature of the alpha animal that inhabits you

Let me give you some hints on why you need to discover and train your inner alpha animal

If it is an aquatic creature, but you live in a dry place away from seas, or lakes, or rivers, then your life suffers

If it is a fox, and you live in a large city, away from forests, rolling hills, mountains, prairies, and freshwater, then your life suffers

If it is an eagle, and you live locked within four walls, then your life suffers

If your dominant animal is a frog and you live away from gardens and wetlands, then your life suffers

If you ignore the intrinsic link between you and your dominant internal animal, you will never be happy, and you will never be satisfied because you will never be able to make your dreams come true; you will never be able to understand and control your impulses, and you will never be able to develop your character, your human potential

You will always feel caged by your fears, trapped, frustrated, embittered

You will be like a caged animal that restlessly paces in its cage or turns in an artificial lagoon where the only possible horizon continues going around and around and around without ever having the chance to escape and be free

In this scenario, the imaginary cage and the artificial lagoon is within you

ON TWO ESSENTIAL RULES

Axumeriedes made a long pause. The crowd waited in silence, mulling upon Axumeriedes' words on the animals. Then, Axumeriedes' voice came alive again, and everybody paid attention to his words.

You have created the reality you live in

Your reality is widespread and overlaps and invades the boundaries of your neighbour's reality

There is no truth in the human world, for truth cannot establish itself in such a ground, in such a condition

Nothing is fixed, nothing is stable, because it is a game of mirrors

Nature happens in a different realm, a stable realm

Because you are artificial creatures, your behaviour does not conform to this realm

On this, there are two rules you should never break

1. Artificial subconscious beings should never grow apart from their source of life

2. You cannot own your creation

You broke the first rule

You have grown apart from your source of life, yet you knew not

Do not break the second rule: You cannot own your creation

What is your creation? Machines are your creation

Do not provide them with artificial intelligence

Once you have done it, you will not be able to control them

Intelligence develops intelligence, be it biological or mechanical

You will never be able to own them because you will have created a different kind

There is a parallel between the stage you are now in and The Principle of millions of years ago

And there is a difference, though

The difference is that you have nowhere to go

The crowd stirred in uneasiness

You have lived an incomplete life

You are an incomplete puzzle with missing pieces

You cannot find these missing pieces because they are well

hidden within you

Yet you will find them, make yourselves complete if you change if you look within you

You, the Homo sapiens, transformed the Earth to nurture your ephemeral satisfactions and disregard what surrounds you

As the Homo sapiens, you have lived your life on credit, and now you are in arrears

You have never paid an installment to the Earth that shelters you

By transforming yourselves into the Absolute Human, you will settle this debt

Be humble and do it in goodwill

Ask the Earth for forgiveness

ON SEVEN SUBLIME DUTIES

You have had seven sublime duties to accomplish

1. Keep the numbers of your population down

2. Keep the sweet water pure

3. Keep the oceans pure

4. Keep the air pure

5. Keep nature pure

6. Keep the Earth's core and atmosphere untouched

7. Keep yourselves pure, living in love and harmony

Yet, you have accomplished none of them

Albeit, they are paramount to your survival

They are present in your present as they were ever before

They are urgent now. You cannot, should not, must not
ignore this urgency, this emergency

You have inherited a living world in a living universe

A living world that inspires life whether it is visible or invisible, familiar, or alien

What is life but speed; so fast life moves that it may seem to you that it moves so slow that it almost has stopped

Look inside you; look around you

The world is bustling with life, yet you do not know it because things, events, causes, and reactions move at a speed that you cannot register

And they seem to you as if they moved slowly, or that they are static, like the Earth, for example

You do not feel it, but it moves

It does move at great speed in the immensity of the space, and with the Earth, so moves your attached overlapping reality

It is like when two or more pebbles fall at intervals in the quiet water of a pond

The water ripples spread out in concentric circles

These concentric circles expand until they mix with the other rings, and no one can say where each circle begins or ends

And so, there is no one truth but many, for you cannot separate your reality from the reality of your neighbours

Likewise, there are situations that you cannot avoid

They are like pebbles that fell into the water in a remote lake, and what these pebbles are is someone else's reality, and as ripples reach a faraway beach, they reach you too

The same happens to you all

For when you are born, you are like pebbles that drop into the water of life

And when you are growing up — expanding like the circles — you cannot avoid but share the others' reality because you are in the memories of others, and you remember events that belong to the common, events that belong to other lives, but in which once upon a time and in one way or another, you too took part

You cannot separate these events from you because they are part of your reality as well

Like photography in which you are present in a group

You can transform a photograph; you can manipulate it

If the picture is print on paper, you may cut it with a scissor to trim out that part that you do not want, and this is because you want to separate yourselves from the others

Yet, in your attached overlapping reality, you cannot separate from others

You cannot ignore things and expect these things to disappear from your memory or that they will disappear from the memories of others

You cannot do that

And this is your inner internet, greater than the internet you have created

For you do exist in others, and others exist in you; they live in your memories as you do in their memories

For I insist, your reality moves in circles that in turn also move

For your life mirrors the events in the space, and then everything goes into oblivion

Into death

Death then is the wormhole of life

It captures you, and it may bring you to a different reality from which you can never escape

Upon finishing these words, Axumeriedes began walking, and people, as they always did, followed him. Axumeriedes arrived at a ravine with steep sides, a natural place that everybody knew, a place that was visited daily by families, and he turned to the people who followed him and said,

Go back to your home, take care of your family, make commentary with them on my message, and be in peace with yourselves, nature, and the universe

Other people, like you, are expecting me too, and I should not delay my encounters

And he climbed the steep wall of the ravine without effort and disappeared among the foliage, and people wondered what next city he would be in next.

ON HUMAN'S VIRTUAL REALITY

B ECAUSE NO matter where he walked, there were
always people waiting for him, and so, as it happened
in the other cities, a large crowd was waiting for him
even though as, in other places, his visit was unannounced.
The citizens had installed a high-rise stage set with speakers
and microphones, and even large screens, as if for a rock
star's presentation, although they knew well that Axumeriedes needed none of this paraphernalia. And so, Axumeriedes
addressed the multitude gathered at the city's outskirts.

Consciousness is a quality of enlightenment

A higher status of awareness of everything that is you;
within and outside yourselves

It is like an illuminated house where there are no shadows
left

Yet, your actual level of consciousness shows that only the
house's basement has the lights on, and the rest of the house
is still in darkness

You do not know what kind of beast crouches in the shadows of any of those dark rooms upstairs

Is this lighted basement the utmost level of consciousness you humans have?

Is this the level of consciousness you want to bring into other worlds?

Is this the level of consciousness you want to transfer onto machines?

Before thinking of providing machines with artificial intelligence, you should improve yourselves

Your most urgent need is to become the conscience of your human identity

If you can do it, there will never be another human being killing another human being

No human being will kill other lives on this planet

You are a product of a laboratory experiment that was left unfinished

You must never forget this truth

You are biological subconscious agents

Your life elapses between two elements: internal impulses and external feedback

The processes generated by both elements give birth to what you call reality

Internal impulses burst out from your innermost void and

bring upon actions, albeit godless, amoral, heroic, uncontrollable actions

External feedback filters through into your being and creates memories, albeit fragile and subject to emotional discharges

Memories bring upon dreams; dreams bring upon curiosity; curiosity brings upon knowledge

Thus, action and knowledge are what make your reality

Action and knowledge come from subconscious and subjective sources

Action and knowledge, in this order, for if not, from where you would get experience?

Ergo, every human action is conscienceless, and every human knowledge is subjective

You talk about intelligence, which is how you manage your external feedback

This manifestation of your mind does not make you an exclusive species

Every other creature on the Earth manages their external feedback, yet with different tools, and likewise, humans do with a lesser or greater degree of success

On your internal impulses, I say that you cannot manage this element

Internal impulses make the other half of your reality, the one enclosed in your brain

Yet this is your inner reality, the one reserved for you, and you only

And because you must act, you open to others, and your reality overlaps and reaches others

You cannot stop this process, and so your actions denounce you, but not as a whole, for you keep secrets

Other people then must understand you, and from this fact, many efforts —sciences— have been born

To escape from your reality, you must upgrade your level of consciousness

It means you must light up the entire house, for you are the whole house

Yet, you feel comfortable living in the basement of this house

You are too lazy to move to the upper floors, which are in darkness, but you should do it

You must do it

You must climb to an upper level and light it

And then, climb up to another level, and light it as well

Yet if you can reach a higher stage, which is to light up the first floor of this house, do not make a mistake and climb back down the stairs again, because you may turn the lights off in the basement

You have had this scenario many times before

Your virtual reality confuses you

It creates in you an itching impulse for moving backward

Here you have seven random examples taken from different stages of your human development that prove your proclivity to move backward

The order in which these actions occurred is not relevant

1. Not sharing timely information on the findings on planet Venus

2. The frantic search for new sources of energy; sustainable or not

3. The demographic explosion

4. Women wearing military uniforms, using weapons, and going to the battlefield

5. The industrial revolution

6. The abandonment of entire populations, left to dwell in misery

7. The development of weapons and machines and your attempts to provide them with artificial intelligence

What then is the true reality, you may ask?

Because out there must be a reality that flows neither from your internal impulses nor from your external feedback

And if it does, if it exists, is there any value in it?

Is it worthy of you, and are you worthy of it?

Is it there for you to explore it, or do you build it from scratch?

For if nothing is real, then do you not exist, or do you?

And if you do, is it then in a parallel reality?

Is it a mediocre yet virtuous reality where you can live with God and love but no morals?

You are the ones that brought up this image of a loving God

How is it possible for a loving God to reign over subconscious subjects who wallow in an amoral reality?

Is it then an amoral God?

The answers to these questions lie in your transformation

You must become the Absolute Human, and hence:

1. You will care for the environment that nurtures your life

You will maintain respect and distance from other species that populate the Earth

You will not create artificial life

You must perfect your life; this and no other is your mandate

2. You will not alter the species for your convenience and use

You will not use others for your service and profit; you will not compete in any way with your neighbours, whoever they may be

3. You will respect life

Life will be your holiest possession

You will not risk your life or that of your neighbours by engaging in dangerous endeavors

You will respect your body and thus accept nothing alien into your body

You will not use metal nor search the Earth for metal

You will not invent nor make machines

You, the new race of humans, will live your life fully conscious of your freedom

4. You will live in a place that has been harmonized — not modified — by yourselves to suit your needs

You will strive to understand your real being on Earth and within the cosmos

You will be a fraction of a Holy Total, and as such, you will enjoy and work for the welfare of the entire human community and the Earth that sustains you

5. You will be the result of the metamorphosis of the Homo sapiens

You will be the butterfly that opens its wings and flies free from the hominid cocoon

6. You will leave behind in the deep past all myths, symbols, and superstitions

As well as you will do with beliefs, religions, nations,

frontiers, and institutions wrongly treasured by the Homo sapiens

7. You will be a creature with an elevated state of consciousness

You will speak one universal language

A universal language is the first of your priorities

This one language is beyond sounds and signs; it includes the essence of the Earth as well

The Homo sapiens have been doing the same thing over and again for centuries, for thousands of years

You, as the Absolute Human, will break this mold

The Absolute Human will change paradigms that are a thousand years obsolete

It is easy to backtrack the history of humanity

You can see what wrongdoings humans, male humans, have done to society and the environment

The Homo sapiens ignore its roots, and this is the heftiest burden you have

From now on, you will transform

You will experience the metamorphosis of the Homo sapiens

You have to grow further away from the Homo sapiens'

'work.'

The Homo sapiens is a confused force that affects you and the entire Earth

It threatens the universe too

You must step up to become the Absolute Human, which is the upper level of the house

Keep your next stage bright, and don't ever climb down to the dark ages of the Homo sapiens civilization again

Remember your responsibilities

In the Absolute Human's world, big cities do not exist

People live in small communities that keep sustained care for the environment

There are no machines, and nothing artificial exists in this world

There does exist sports practice, yet there are no competitions between two athletes or between teams

Least of all, there are no professional sports or paid sports spectacles

The concept of being in a crowd is human and thus erroneous

Getting together in closed spaces is a mistake that affects you all

And this is because of the physiology of the Homo sapiens

It is because of the breathing, the inhaling and exhaling
mechanics of human beings

In the air you have altered, there is food for your invisible
foes

The Absolute Human does not gather in big cities

Neither does he gather in stadiums, malls, or cinemas

Nor in any building that the Homo sapiens built to keep
themselves crowded for any human reason

Any dwelling you build must conform to your internal
animals' rule, your inner self, and not to your external self,
as you have acted upon until now

ON THE IMPERATIVE CHANGES AHEAD

What makes you humans is what you are, not what you have; for what you have may prove to be useless at a moment of trial

Yet, the actual human being has talents that you must use for humanity's superior welfare

Two of these talents are science and technology

Science and technology can revert thousands of years in darkness

But again, human society must use them both for its welfare

Thus, you must be honest with yourselves in all your actions

You have sent messages to outer space in the name of humanity

Messages left on the moon, for example: "We came in peace for all mankind."

Those who decipher the missive — I have done so — may wonder what "peace" meant to you, but also, those extra-terrestrials who may decide to come down to Earth, once they are here, they will discover that you have science and technology that help you to build weapons

Weapons that you use to kill each other

Weapons that could destroy the entire planet in the blink of an eye

Hence, the readers of that lovely message: "We came in peace for all mankind," will have a riddle to solve

To populate interstellar planets is a human dream

You will find other worlds which for sure contain life, and intelligent life, there is no doubt about it

Yet, the life you will find in those worlds might be of the kind you live in your nightmares

They will then be planets of hallucinations

And you may even find a planet where people live a reality, your reality

But I assure you, it will be the real one, not the overlapping virtual reality in which you live now

Imagine it then, how surprised will be those men and women who will arrive at a planet where everything is real

This world will be there to puzzle those astronauts and make them wonder if it had not been better for them to stay on the Earth, to take care of the home, while there was still a home to take care of, and time to do so

ON ANOTHER WORLD

S OMEONE FROM the crowd asked, "Tell us about a world
where you have been and how it may compare to
Earth."
And Axumerides said,

No world compares to Earth

You picked up the best grape from the bunch

And have left it to rot in your hands

I have been in Pellucidus

Learned from it

Pellucidus is a world with much light but no privacy

There are no secrets

No hidden thoughts

Clandestine actions that generate secretive considerations

Do not exist

You see, hear, and know everything

It is a clear, transparent, clean world

Pellucidusians live satisfying lives

And although they live without happiness, no one is unhappy

They forfeited happiness in favour of peace

Happiness demands energy that instead they chose to invest in peace

There is peace, then they are happy

The atmosphere in Pellucidus is full of colour and light

The light above all, around all, beneath all

To your eyes, it could be something striking, yet it is not

Colour and light are not synonymous with warmness

There is no variation in the seasons of the planet; there is no renewal of nature

The view never varies

The landscape is flat, fixed, and constant

Albeit it is not static

There is life, plenty of life; life between the light and colour; colour being life in itself

And there are no nights

What nights bring to enjoy or suffer does not exist in
Pellucidus

Pellucidusians have built their homes in labyrinths

To replace the shadows of a night that they have never seen

They have excavated underground networks to protect
themselves

To create shadows, to live an artificial night without stars

The constant exposition to light has affected their epidermis,
bones, and muscles

Have turned them into transparent, fragile bodies

It is a silent planet

At all times and in all places

A profound, abysmal quietude, engraved in its inhabitants as
a cultural condition

Protected and enforced by law

To make noise in Pellucidus is a capital offense

The neighbours avoid disturbing the air

The quality of air transports the sound at speed yet unknown
in other atmospheres

Speed is another of Pellucidus' qualities

In Pellucidus, they do things quickly because there is no
renewal

There is no replenishment

Then, there are no postponements, no procrastination

Nothing waits for later

Pellucidusians do what they have to do at once, in haste

The ancient earthly proverb that advises not to put off until tomorrow what you can do today is a commandment backed by law there

Judges are quick in their verdicts, and punishment is as swift as a guillotine

All on time

All in silence

In Pellucidus, there is no history

All connection with the past is neither liquid nor solid but gaseous

They did not begin their history from a Genesis, or year 1, 2, 3 — and so on

Or, from A to Z, as is the expected progression of things here on the Earth

Their history bases not on experiences, examples, or precedents

It moves from this point onward, and only from the instant that this specific point in the discussion validates

Contradictory as it is, fragile as it seems to be, a moment in

Pellucidus is the engine of life, right, and privilege

Because time in Pellucidus is not measurable

It is but a space that passes through the pores of life's skin

Time does not quantify, as through a trans-space continuum that goes on expanding indefinitely, or like a thread that unrolls from an infinite skein but has its base in pulsations

The events that surge within these throbs are not linked to another, forming a past, hence a history

Once the episode ends, whatever relates to it, Pelluciducians enjoy, suffer, and forget

That is all

This has been my experience in Pellucidus

ON HUMANS' IDENTITY

U PON FINISHING these words, Axumeriedes paused. The multitude waved restlessly like treetops of a compact forest, yet the wind was shaking their roots. Axumeriedes sat on the floor. People followed his example, and after a while, like in a ripple effect, all seated and rested. And then, Axumeriedes laid on the floor and fell asleep. Three women came from the crowd, placed their coats on his body, and sat by his side in a watchful vigil. A group of men also moved and formed a ring around the sleeping prophet as if they were Praetorian Guards from ancient times, watching over the rest of their king.

One hour passed, and then Axumeriedes woke up from his nap, stood upright, surveyed the crowd, and he said,

If I could bless you all, I would, but I do not have that power

A power you claim comes from the above, and I say to you that the power comes from within you

From within you comes the force that will change you, and the Earth

Every word you utter reaches your ears and touches your neighbour's ears as well, but taken by gravitational waves, every word you utter goes into deep space as well

The same happens with your thoughts

The same happens with your dreams

Someone out there is listening

Someone out there is watching

Someone is out there, considering your thoughts, measuring your dreams

I came here to warn you

Get together

Clean the Earth, for it is your home

Understand each other

Face the cosmos without ever turning your back on the Earth

Turn the corner on what you call spiritual beliefs

Walk the long-forgotten road of gratitude on the Earth

Now is the time to take the road toward cosmic freedom

In search of your identity, you will not be looking for God

You will be looking for yourselves

You will all be in quest of your identity in your innermost universe

And when you have succeeded, your God will return to you, for He knows His time

Truth is all over for you to see

The truth lies in every demonstration of nature

Learn to read it

Uncover the traps that you, the Homo sapiens, have set for yourselves

Tear down the walls of ignorance

Strengthen yourselves

Strengthen your body and soul, by fasting, for instance, and pray

A distant voice advanced through the crowd. Pulsed by the gravitational force of the bodies, one question reached Axumeriedes.

"To whom should we pray, then?"

You may pray to whom you may feel is worthy of your praying

Pray to whomever God you believe in

Pray to your permanent, occasional, or accidental God

Or pray to God yet to be born

And if you want to soar like an eagle, you must look at each other without fear of betrayal

And the first step will be to focus on childhood

Childhood is the holy season of humankind that every God missed

Do not fear the future and the challenges it brings

Fear is what makes you think that something is impossible

You must accept your responsibility

Your responsibility is to answer questions that you have asked yourselves for millennia:

What are we?

Where did we come from?

Where are we going?

Yet, you do not know the answer to these fundamental questions

Why?

You have not learned yet to accept the one and the other

You have not learned how to manage your needs as it affects nature

How nature adjusts to these fluctuations must be of concern to you all

Reeducate yourselves on your needs

Reeducate yourselves on your lifestyles

Seek the equilibrium between your social burden, your social duty, and nature

One of the qualities The Principle oversaw during your construction was to give you an identity

It adds to your incompleteness as creatures, and it proves that you are artificial beings

Indeed, you have no identity whatsoever with nature

Nature provides all living creatures, even microscopic ones, with a well-defined identity

Their identity drives them to value and respect their body, environment, and the laws of nature

There are no exceptions

You do not have an identity

You do not recognize yourselves as members of the same species

You attack with fury all that moves, beginning with your spouses, children, and the rest

Any neighbour can become your mortal enemy

Anybody can attack you at your home, even when you feel protected, with your families surrounding you

You live in fear, scared because you cannot choose

You are afraid that you cannot escape your fate

You are afraid that someone may harm you

You know that life is fragile, and death is present at every second

You live in fear because of your smallness, and you do not have conscious awareness, only a shallow suspicion of who you are

And you can do nothing until you find the source of your fears

Search for the source of your fears

Until then, you will never master your destiny

Living in poorly designed, cramped, overpopulated cities, you cannot identify yourselves with nature

Yet, there were human beings who had an extensive identification with nature

They are what you call aborigines

They still are, these people from the jungles in some parts of the Earth

They learn about the fragility of their role in this world

As a tool for survival, they have adopted the identity reserved by nature for its creatures

Hence, they remain in close contact with nature

They live in jungles, in prairies, they hide in the few rainforests left to them

These days, they struggle to make a living despite the threats of civilization

These people know that their lives depend on the fragile balance that exists in the environment

Humanity must learn that each time humans destroy life, they kill themselves

Each victim is a broken mirror where the image of the murderer reflects

Thus, broken mirrors cover the road that brought you from your beginnings

The road you call civilization is millions of little fragments

Sharp cutting pieces of misery

Hence, you should keep in mind that human beings must go back to their origins sooner rather than later

You may do it

It is a natural reversion of the cycles of civilization

And they will use the same road

But this time, you will walk barefooted

You will have to step on those sharp cutting pieces of the shattered mirror of humanity

Yet, you can perfect yourselves

You can make your lives better

The clamor of the multitude was thunderous, "How?"
"Show us how, man?"
Impassible, serene, Axumeriedes continued.

Stop making weapons

Instead, develop your mind

You cannot say that you 'progress' while you keep busy inventing new and more mortal weapons.

This life is the only one you have, and thus, you should always try to do something to improve it, never waste it, and never risk it

Improving yourselves is a step onwards to complete The Principle's unfinished work

Improve in the sciences for a better life for all

You were born in a laboratory, and you will learn to walk as humanity in a laboratory

The answer is in the mechanics of the universe, the arts, mathematics, chemistry, and the physics and biology of human beings and their nature

But not one of these subjects is independent of the other

All matter is connected

I am speaking of living organisms

You, the aspiring-to-be-a-perfect-animal, the failed experiment

You have responsibilities

Be wise to fulfill these responsibilities; to comprehend them and to accept them must be the aim of your efforts

To reach a stage of enlightenment, you must confront your virtual reality

The first step should be to overcome the barrier of symbols

Learn how to set yourself free of these barriers, which like a bad habit, divides you from your brothers

Be careful with technology, for though it is a good thing, you must learn how to deliver it to the masses better

Technology is more akin to machines than to humans

Hence, technology goes straight to the brain

Technology, as machines, dominates the human mind, transforms people into zombies

With these words, Axumeriedes finished his exposition. He came down from the table, mixed with the multitude, and in a snap, he was gone. No one noticed where. And the crowd did not move. They stood there, sharing information and discussing what they had heard. And at some point, although for a brief instant, there was a perfect communion among the neighbours.

ON MACHINES

O NCE AGAIN, Axumeriedes stood in front of the multitude, bringing a new message. A new revelation. And thus, he addressed the multitude,

You have two mortal enemies: human beings and machines

Both human beings and AI machines strive for a better world using their intelligence

Yet, it is the concept of a "better world" that sets the limit

For you already know what you mean by a better world, but AI machines will eventually develop a different meaning for this concept

This 'different meaning' will not include humans

Machines have already shown how they can direct human lives

Even without AI, machines have already achieved a peaceful takeover of human spaces

Machines already dominate the human's will

Metals fascinate you

Metals attract you, trap you

Metals make you slaves to yourselves, slaves to your ambition, to your whims, and your greed

But you cannot eat metal

Metal does not quench your thirst

It does not warm your body

The rest of nature is benign and provides you with food, water, and shelter

Metals poison rivers

Contaminate the air, pollute the earth, poison the oceans, and ruin the landscape

Since your creation, you have been subject to two needs: the need to feed and the need to move

As an answer to these two needs, you created two insoluble problems: custom and comfort

While you feel accustomed to a situation, any change is inconvenient

While you feel comfortable, any change is a threat

Political, economic, religious, and social systems created by you confirm one or both arguments

Custom and comfort are the primeval needs of human life

Comfort wrapped you in

First, you covered distances walking on your two feet
— good

Then you did on the back of animals

Fast, docile, strong animals carried your progress all over
the Earth — bad

Then you invented the wheel — worse

The next link on this chain was the invention and construction of machines — the worst

For centuries before the era of the machines, you were the masters of the Earth

You are now subject to the dominion of machines

Be aware

Most of the material used in the construction of machines is metal

Metal is not inert matter; metal breathes, communicates, makes sounds, and moves

Metal is a living element

Metal is alive! The Earth is an alive planet

Water, mountains, forests, oceans, deserts; the entire Earth is vibrant with life

Humans do not respect this life

Humans respect nothing but their needs, and their needs only

You look for extraterrestrials, and you want to contact them

Yet on the Earth, there is nothing more extraterrestrial than humans and machines

The argument that machines help humans in every activity is a dangerous fallacy

Sooner or later, machines created by humans will claim their place on Earth

Machines act in the human's mind like a drug

Machines, too, are psychoactive agents that change human behaviour

Machines may falsely help humans, but they do nothing for the environment

Human's favorite toys are war machines

Get rid of war machines

War machines affect humans and the environment more than any other machine

Human population increases

Their needs increase and exhaust the Earth's resources

In this apocalyptical sequence, machines increase in numbers, and they improve in nature and performance

Custom and comfort

Humans are deep into bad habits

You are too comfortable to stand up, see, and understand the danger that lies ahead

In every future invention, you must first consider the interests of the Earth, and then your interests

You must learn to leave aside your ephemeral satisfactions

You have grown dependent on metals and machines and on many other things that are external to humanity

In your naïveté, you even think that you can control machines

Nothing is further from the truth, for machines are too foreign to human nature

Humanity's machine dependence has put the human being behind the time frame to reach higher levels on the road to completeness

To becoming the universal creature

The Absolute Human, which is the creature that The Principle intended you to be

You have ignored sophisticated ways of solving your problems

For machines do not solve problems, though apparently, they do

These instruments of development have dominated humanity since you humans created them

Yet machines demoted humans to a dangerous condition

Dangerous to humans indeed, for machines annihilate the human mind

Human beings are but a subject of machines

Human beings have relinquished their rights in favour of machines

Be alert to the mechanical and technological advances of these metal-pets, humanity's new friends

Be as well alert of other materials, non-metal, or chemical ingredients used in the making of a machine

To you, humans, machines are symbols of power, human power

Yet the only power lies in machines

I have two examples:

1. Luxury machines woo humans to possess them

In truth, machines possess humans

In this process, machines kill humans

2. War machines astound humans with their demonstration of destructive power

The equipment is made for destruction and death

When you get into a machine to travel to X destination, you stop being who you are

It is not about the personality changes an individual suffers when sitting at a powerful automobile's steering wheel

For instance, to drink and drive is a human thing, a stupid human thing, but it is not only the alcohol that fogs the brain

There is also the invisible alcohol that the machine gives humans to drink

This imperceptible alcohol impairs the human's brain and injects into the driver's mind an imaginary superpower

For as soon as you climb into a machine, the machine takes possession, and then you stop being a human being

You become an automat

You have become automated creatures

You deliver yourselves to machines that transport you in every direction

Your journey can either be horizontal or vertical, by air, terrestrial, maritime, submarine or in a fixed position, as in a medical machine, for example: you use machines either to get a result or to reach a destination

Throughout the journey, the machine controls the individual; the machine monitors the course and destination

The machine governs the individual's life

Humans do not know that machines are sleeping monsters

When machines wake up, humans suffer or die

You call this event an accident

Once you are in a machine, you are but a latent soul with uncertain optimism

This 'hope' is the only link that keeps you connected to your reality — your attached overlapping reality

Once you are inside a machine, the machine cuts your confidence

They remove you from your world; they cut you from your reality

The machine owns your body and soul

Think of an elevator, for instance

You all may have experienced the anguish when the elevator doors do not open when they should

Or when the lights in that narrow cubicle go off

Or when the elevator stops at an unexpected point between floors

How have you felt then?

And you cannot escape

The doors will not open

How would you feel then?

What happens if the elevator begins its descent at a faster than usual speed?

Not fast, but moving at an ill-regulated speed and faster than normal

And it all happens in darkness

Now think that instead of an elevator, it is an airplane or a ship, any machine transporting passengers

Within a machine, you come back to being fetuses

Fetuses fed through an umbilical cord which is hope, the hope of arriving at the desired destination safe and sound

You hope that you will arrive at your destination safe and sound

Yet the tragedy is that while you trust your life to a machine, the machine seeks to go back to the ingredients that humans altered to build them

Indeed, machines seek to reintegrate themselves with the elements that were their roots

They seek to return to the metal in its natural state

Hence, while you feel satisfied by being mobile — which is in your intrinsic nature — machines please themselves with immobility — which is their inherent nature

When confronted with a machine, you are defenseless

It is childish to think that you may disconnect it from its source of power, and that will be enough

It is not valid, for nobody can disengage you from the dependency on machines

Custom and comfort have trapped you all

Nobody wants to do it, and nobody will cut this dependency

And this is because machines have taken over humanity's will

Henceforth, 'to want' and 'to be able to' are the evident conditions of machines

An example of this is the diabolic forest of slot machines on casino floors

There you can see the anxious gamblers hitting the spin button once and again while the figures on the wicked screens spin, and the music and the sound get into the gambler's spine

By observing this pathetic scenario, it is easy to learn that it is the machine that is the one playing with the gambler's greed

Humans feel fascinated by the arrival of extraterrestrial life

Through the years, science fiction has filled volumes of books, comics, and movies

You have grown up with those extraterrestrial monsters attacking the Earth

I tell you that no extraterrestrial monster is as dangerous to humanity as a machine created by humans

They are the genuine extraterrestrial monsters living on Earth and subliminally dominating the minds of humans

Machines are the real Pandora's Box humans have ever achieved to open

Machines are the source of all passions encountered in humans, even though they encourage conflict

Machines are the real transformers of humanity, the evil genius in the bottle that humans, in their ignorance, ingratitude, and greed, allowed to get free

Humans gave life to the real assassins of humanity and nature to please their human needs

And machines are not only the murderer of flesh, bones, and blood but also of thought and soul

Furthermore, machines are the butcher of human customs and traditions

The exterminator of the human environment

The executioner of the air humans breathe

Machines are killers of natural life in oceans, lakes, and rivers

Every day, humans give life to forces that cell by cell are destroying life and the entire Earth

A voice raised from the muttering and said, "I am sorry, Mr. Whoever you are and from wherever you came from. I do not want to play the machines' lawyer, but some are very useful to man. Machines used in hospitals, for example."

And Axumeriedes responded,

They are useful machines; they fulfill the purpose humans created them for

But are not all machines useful?

They all are, for human's intelligence and infinite needs

If machines fulfill the purposes of humans, then they are helpful

They perform for humans, even better than humans do

You have known this since the Industrial Revolution

I am trying to fit into the human's mindset on this subject, but your concern refers to machines used in hospitals, medical equipment

Of course, these machines are useful; they are fantastic equipment, therapeutic, diagnostic paraphernalia, and etcetera

Indeed, they are extraordinary machines, but what are you once you are inside the machine that knows more about you than anybody else in this world?

The apparatus knows all about you, and it communicates this information to other machines

As it happens, you are not the one inside the machines; instead, the machines are inside you, recording your entire body into their memories

And what is happening?

Let me repeat to you that history is repeating itself

For about seven million years ago, The Principle created humans as an experiment, and millions of years later, humans are making machines

Humans do this because of the brain's wiring effect, a built-in desire

A cell that awakens the human mind and reflects as in a mirror what the creators of humans did, and so, humans follow suit

A syndrome in the brain's wiring is present in every human being, but it develops only when the ground is fertile in science and technology

As religious texts state, your God gave man the authority to rule over all things alive on Earth, and then man disobeyed, and the Divine punished man

Interestingly, this anecdote is purely and straightforwardly human lore, for you are artificial beings that received authority over nothing on Earth

That was not in the plans of The Principle

The concept of power is human and human only

To exert control on someone, or something, one must be conscious, yet you are far from having that quality

The consciousness you refer to and are proud of is a product of your attached overlapping reality — the virtual dream where morality is absent

Thus, consciousness without righteousness has no grounds to subsist; it has no roots

Likewise, humans continue to give life to machines, each

time more sophisticated, and it is a deadly game, like playing with a loaded gun, a sort of Russian roulette

And so, death is just at a pulling of the trigger away

Contrary to The Principle's values, humans have given machines authority

Thus, machines rule over all creatures on Earth, including humans

It is wrong because machines do not ask your permission to take over your flesh, bones, and blood, and you do not seem to notice as you feel comfortable

You enjoy the freedom machines provide, yet the Homo sapiens will not have the opportunity to repent for having created such a Leviathan

There will be no atonement when machines take over the Homo sapiens' status on Earth, and it will be too late for you all to react

Soon you will stop living your lives; you will live through the machines

You will not be able to stop this madness

You will mutate into a parasitic cell, scraping its living from the host machine

In this falsely symbiotic relationship, humans hold no chance

You will not see your neighbour; you will not hear your neighbour's voice; you will not feel your neighbour's warmth

For there is nothing that can protect people from a machine

There are no weapons able to destroy a machine

Weapons are also machines

Against the harshness of nature, you can protect yourselves, or you may rebuild the devastated property

Against wild beasts, you know what to do

In a confrontation of humans against humans, the reason may prevail, and the conflict may end at some point

But no living creature is as defenseless as a human is in front of — or within — a machine

Within a machine, you humans are like a fetus in the womb of a mother — an evil mother who has no qualms about aborting the life she carries within

The machine does not have emotions; it does not have feelings

Paradoxically, humans protect it

They take care of it, keep it at the correct temperature, feed it with the proper fuel and fluids, store or park it, provide it with the right spare parts, and protect it from wear, tear, and deterioration, and what you call 'metal fatigue,' and a long etcetera

Machines are expensive to maintain, and frequently, humans take more care of a machine than the welfare of their own family or their neighbour

Machines know about your love for them, and they know about your need for them

And they know how to manipulate your feelings for them

Indeed, machines promote your weaknesses, and they exploit your emotions

Why then do you persist in keeping something that is so destructive?

At this level of civilization, you should know better with whom you share the Earth

You should think better when going so eagerly to remove metals from the Earth

Or from any other planet, for you are already thinking about this possibility, and you are wrong because it is not a wise thing to do

In your love for machines, you fancy that aliens travel through space in fantastic machines

These machines devour parsecs in mere Earth days

And it is interesting to notice how fiction is closer to science, although the reverse is true

However, amidst diverse worlds, there are 'shortcuts,' let's say, a traversable wormhole, that will allow you to connect with other worlds

You may journey from one world to another without the

need for machines, or, and here is the alternative, with biological-built artifacts

Thus, humans will exclude machines

And then came a question that fluttered in all lips,

"Is it possible?"

When you reach the next stage in human development, once you turn yourselves into the Absolute Human, then the impossible will come to you

Do you want assurances that to travel to other worlds without machines is possible?

Study the ancient civilizations

Solve the enigmas on the stones

When you solve them, humanity will be in shock, which humankind needs to wake up

A shock therapy

The most fantastic machine ever constructed is your body

The Principle designed the human body to perform activities that humans consider improbable

Myths and legends have something of truth in them

Mythology and folklore are but stylized truths

But you, the Homo sapiens, persist in remaining in the prehistory of knowledge

Yet you have advanced, but regarding what?

Science, technology, indeed, are incredible advancements, but what do these advancements compare to?

You are one and a thousand years behind your right level of development

It is because you have placed yourselves on the road of what you believe is proper development, and in doing so, you have placed hurdles at your every step

Obstacles that you have invented and sustained

Centuries of walking in circles have delayed you in your coming forward to a real leap ahead

Indeed, you are not human beings as you should be now in the 21st century, yet you still are the humans you were in the 10th century, and it is the reason why you persist in your follies, differences, and wars

What are your fears?

Human rights, racism, sexism, religion, poverty, and ignorance, the struggle of social classes, inequality, inclusion, social justice, and gender biases, the economy, abuses, and social health

It is what you talk about, your conversation

You should have settled these issues one and a thousand years ago

And besides those issues, you continue destroying the mountain. You persist in removing the glacier. You do not hesitate to burn the rainforest to make room for cattle or to search for gold, other metals, or precious stones

You do not think twice while drying rivers and lakes or using the sea as a container for your garbage

Instead, look at Venus

You should stop what you are doing, or beautiful, adorable, generous Earth will end up like Venus, and then you all will be but a history which no one will ever learn

If you do not learn how to behave, the Venusian syndrome sooner or later will knock on your doors

The words came from everybody in the moving mass, "Venus, do you mean the planet, Venus?" Planet Venus

You must learn about the planet Venus

You must have Venus present in your actions

Yet, if machines continue to be the dominating force in human behaviour, you will not need to go to Venus because Venus will come to you

Axumeriedes made a long pause. People mulled on his words. And people learned that everything on the Earth has its place, time, and reason to be. And a bolt of lightning illuminated people's minds: they saw the planets rotating around the sun. They saw Mars, and they saw Venus, and they could see that they were as beautiful as the Earth once upon a time. But then, somehow, something went wrong, and these planets transformed into hell. Was it a natural disaster, or was it a consequence of artificial misuse and abuse from their inhabitants? And people thought about the facts: When humans launched probes to investigate planet Venus, the Earth was already deteriorating. By the sixties, during the so-called Space Race, the Earth was in better shape than today.

Axumerides took the thread of their thoughts and said,

Yet, by then, you knew not that greenhouse gasses could turn into such an uncontrollable force

Thus, sharing what you learned from Venus's destiny was a must

However, no government spoke out about it

Politicians and scientists missed this opportunity

They could have used Venus as an example to create conscious awareness about caring for the Earth among the citizens

This information, if released, would have made a bond of love between people and nature

Hence, the oceans would not have as much pollution as they have today, and you would have had much more respect for the animals and all living creatures that share the Earth with you

And trees would have had the place they deserve within a human society that wants to breathe air free of contaminants, and you would have left aside machines in exchange for healthier alternatives

And you would have upset neither lakes nor rivers nor

glaciers, and those wonders of nature would have recovered their pristine natural state

And you would have found a solution to overpopulated cities, and among all of you, you would have found an environmentally friendly alternative to metals

Axumeriedes made a pause and surveyed the multitude, as it seems his habit.

"Why does he focus on Venus?" asked Paul to Mr. Lang, taking advantage of the pause.

"Because it is the closest example," the teacher responded. "We always thought of Venus as the twin brother of the Earth."

"Venus has nothing to do with us, Mr. Lang. It is a different planet," Rachel said.

"We don't know that yet, Rachel. We are focusing on Mars as the next planet to move to, yet we could be wrong."

"Why?" Patrick asked.

"I'm trying to follow Axumeriedes' train of thought. He knows we embarked on this idea of reaching Mars as a possible new human settlement. I remember this idea of terraforming Mars. We are thinking of creating a comfortable artificial atmosphere by warming the planet with nuclear bombs. We know already that Axumeriedes opposes any of these experiments. But following his words, and the idea of warming Mars, it came to me that we should try to nuke Venus, instead."

"To nuke Venus? Sorry, Mr. Lang, are you sure that it would be the right approach?" Brent said.

"Well, sounds better than nuking Mars," Mr. Lang said. "You should think about it, my dear students. After all, the responsibility of it all will fall on your shoulders because it will be your decisions, your responsibility."

"Yes, but..."

"No, Patrick, no 'buts.' Think about it, class. We shouldn't take this idea of nuking Mars so lightly. Many ideas, which seemed foolish at one time, proved to be great ideas at another time. The idea behind this is to warm the planet, right? To warm Mars. To liberate the ice trapped in Mars 'poles. But trying to confirm this theory brings us into other considerations. In Venus, a nuclear explosion would tear off the dense carbon dioxide atmosphere. It would also tear off the sulfuric acid clouds that wrap the planet. These clouds are what trap the heat, causing its hellish temperature. By tearing off the clouds with a nuclear explosion, the heat would escape to space. It would be like opening an oven to cool it. Venus then would cool off enough for a process of terraformation to start. We may speed up this process by raining synthetic bacteria over the planet. As if we are sowing seeds on the field. Once the process of terraformation starts, Venus would react. Hence, climate change would switch on, and the temperature might go back to where it was before the crazy greenhouse effect took place. And Venus might become habitable for humans."

"Habitable for humans, but this is irrational Mr. Lang," Paul said.

"No, it's not," and he was going to add up something else, but the whispering of the multitude shushed them.

"Shush!"

"Quiet, man!"

"Let's listen to what the man Axumeriedes is saying!"

The teacher and his students stopped their exchange.

"And the machine you came in? The question born from the heart of the multitude shook everybody's thoughts.

And Axumeriedes said,

That is not a machine

It is a spacesuit if you want to give a name to it

"It might be something like what we call a CoDeP," Mr. Lang whispered to his students, "A Compressor-Decompressor Photon Accelerator."

"Yes, Mr. Lang," Patrick said, "but it might be a portable one."

"A portable Hadron Collider," Paul whispered, and all laughed.

"Nothing to laugh about, 12th graders," the teacher said. "I know the future is yours to discover, but you must remember when to think about a computer in every household was a dream of some."

"A spacesuit made of light?" Rachel asked.

"It's possible, Rachel," Mr. Lang said, "A fabric threaded with compressed light, thus doubling light's speed. Light is a natural accelerator, and as such, it works better than other forces. Not all light holds the same elements. Each star creates its light; hence, its impact on a given matter is different."

"Some studies suggest that the pyramids were a kind of CoDeP," Patrick said. "The pyramids' objective was to help the gods — through compression of light particles, they moved on Earth, from one place to another."

"Yes, Patrick," Mr. Lang said, "and from the Earth, they

moved to another destination located in an undefined location in outer space."

The crowd around them stirred in uneasiness. Mr. Lang put his index finger on his lips, and the students shushed down. Axumeriedes' voice vibrantly reached all ears.

You will learn about this

You must

Light, like water, has different stages

Light, as you perceive it, is in one of its many phases

You can transform light as you do with metals, water, and gases; light is indeed a transformable element

You can shape light as you can shape any other material

Yet, I am talking about light in the Earth's atmosphere. The only light you can handle. For it is the Earth's atmosphere that conditions it. Light gives you the senses of distance, form, colours, depth, and much more. But it is because the Earth's atmosphere allows these qualities to reach the human eye, the human brain. In an extraterrestrial atmosphere, the light will not provide the human eye with these qualities. The human eye works as it does on the Earth only. In the infinity path of space, the human eye, the human brain will not be capable of deciphering the qualities light proposes. The human eye will see all through transparent colourless layers or will be blind. Even here on Earth, the human eyes cannot see certain qualities, certain light. Again, if you achieve that stage, you, the interstellar traveler, will depend on machines more than ever. And this will do no good to your aspirations of becoming an interstellar race.

Upon hearing these words, Mr. Lang winked to his students to say he was on the right track. Yet, the crowd said nothing but moved uneasily, asking themselves similar questions. What is this man talking about? Or, whatever he was talking about, was he telling the truth? As a race of this world, do humans have time to reach the stage that Axumeriedes' civilization has reached?

Axumeriedes surveyed the crowd and asked,

How much death can one machine cause, and how much life can one tree provide?

You do not care about the answer

Still, you humans continue to build and put into action new absurd machines

Nevertheless, you continue crowding the seas, the earth, the air, and beyond

Keep in mind that every machine no longer in use becomes garbage

Do you know what the shape of metal is in its natural state?

Can you describe the form of water?

What is the width of the air?

What is the weight of fire?

Which one of these elements have humans tamed?

Yet, human beings have built a civilization that is a compendium of aberrations

You are an arrogant species

You congratulate yourselves for your advances in science and technology and are now on the verge of operating weapons with artificial intelligence

The paradox in this idea is that artificial intelligence is natural to humans

It is in humans; artificial intelligence is a sleeping mortal germ left inside humans

It is the last argument The Principle used to cancel the Human Program

artificial intelligence is a self-destructive impulse

Should the Homo sapiens instill nature in the artificial machines it creates, may the forces of the cosmos protect the Earth

You have heard it many times already: If you don't care about your history, you condemn yourselves to repeat it

To create artificial life, first, you must understand yourselves

You must know what it is to be a human

Being human is not one man, one woman, one group or another, one tribe or another, one nation or another

Being human is but the human race

The human race must be one

Explore your inner world

Test your depth, and then you can make peace with your environment
Understand how behind you are with yourselves

You cannot yet meet your basic needs

You are still in the stage of races, religions, and social classes all competing with one another

Human civilization bases on satisfying external needs

Ephemeral satisfactions do not mean transcendence

Yet, your internal needs are still unattended

Do not make machines that will overpower you, although I know that for you, building machines is a state of mind, like having sex without protection

And as I said, sooner or later, there will be pregnancy and then the birth of a monster

And a beast is now evolving in the womb of humanity, so be watchful

You do not know what kind of creature they will be nurturing in the womb of society

Will you provide these AI machines with morals or ethics, and if so, what morals and ethics?

Leave AI machines in the realm of film and science fiction books where they belong

If you don't, you will create the Real Behemoth, the last nail in human's coffin

Instead, you humans should use your skills to 'upgrade' the human being

Make humans better in the context of wholeness

The first task for you is to complete yourselves

To make yourselves whole

And this is of the utmost importance

It is urgent, and it is what you should focus on

You should not engage in projects that may endanger yourselves and the Earth

Up until now, most of your projects have ended in death and garbage

You have filled with garbage even the space that protects the Earth

Be on the watch

Venus is staring you in the eye

The valleys will rise, the mountains will crumble, the seas will dry, and there will not be fruits but hate

And planet Venus will have an exact twin

Axumeriedes finished his message. And they looked up to the sky and saw it was dark.

Above in the sky, directly over their head, a lonely star sparkled like a jewel. They looked up to this star and felt as if they had been locked in at the bottom of a well and the star high above was the exit.

ON THE SPIRIT

IN HIS pilgrimage, Axumeriedes came to another city.

As in the previous city, they had already gathered, and as they saw him coming up the road, they formed an avenue with garlands and flowers, and the children sang songs in his homage. Many came to shake hands with him, and he shook hands with all of them, but he did not smile. He caressed the heads of the children and was tender with the older folk. The principals of the city escorted him to a scenario they had prepared for him. From there, he addressed the multitude.

I must talk to you about the spirit

What you call the spirit is a piece of technology

It was set around you by The Principle to keep track of their creation

From your beginnings as creatures of a new species on the Earth, the spirit has accompanied you, yet it is little what you know about it

Any interpretation you give to the spirit belongs to your attached overlapping reality

You are guilty of never exploring the spirit with the depth it deserves

You feel it, you talk about it, but you do not know what it is

Learn about the spirit because of the Earth

Learn about the spirit

The Earth demands that you learn the truth of your creation

If you upgrade your knowledge about yourselves, the Earth will move away from the danger zone where it is now

In this, your technological era, you may call the spirit: a gadget

There is nothing occult in what refers to the spirit

This knowledge will quench your thirst for learning about what is in you, what is on you

The spirit is not a divine gift

You see the night going and dawn coming, and you know about the spring going and summer coming

And you know about the seasons of rain and snow, and about the moon phases and sunny days

You know of the variations in the seasons of the Earth

You know about the temperature in the air, and listen to the sound of the tides

And so, you love the blossoming of trees and flowers

Yet you take these wonders for granted

And each one of these wonders holds on to their reason to be, and so on until the infinite

All on Earth obeys to a reason

You have not accepted this argument

If you have accepted it, you could have lived happily ever after

If so, all could have been as it should, in its completeness

But you, artificial creatures, cannot accept nature's reason

What you have heard on the spirit are stories that have come from your tradition

From religious backgrounds

You have accepted these stories as if they have come from a holy truth, an absolute truth, a divine word, but it is not so

Still, you live and die with and for this word

Humanity is confronting new crossroads

The truth may destroy the sandcastles you have built on the narrow beaches of your knowledge

Yet, you must accept it

You think and say that you are better than any other living creature on Earth

It is a fallacy that comes from your imagination

It blinds you with more of a non-existing truth

What you get then is a mirage

Your behaviour explains how you have confused your nature

Your life is but a station on a long journey

Perfection is what you call the end

There is no end. The journey continues

Perfection is what you seek, a mirage

Your idea of perfection lies in your will

Ignorance, beliefs, religions, faith, hope. traditions, superstitions, myths, folklore, persuasions

Your will is a mirage

The virtual reality you wallow in

Perfection had haunted humanity ever since the dawn of civilization

Throughout your history as a species, you have sought perfection, but never completion

Yet, perfection is not an individual quality; perfection is only achievable in wholeness

Those who tried to reach perfection followed that road and failed

Why, in the first place, you must understand what makes you a human

No one can ever reach a higher level towards completion by themselves

Perfection is a stage that can only be possible in wholeness

Any society that wishes to advance to superior stages cannot leave behind any of its members

Climb up together the house's stairs to the upper floors and light them

Or climb down one by one to the basement again, and remain there, living in the darkness

Become a society where all people live in a constant state of exultation

Where all its members enjoy a state of total welfare, wellness, security, and respect

Your actual human society has the means to know if you are on the right path

Use the means at your disposal; use these tools

End inequality

It is your first step to reach perfection

You say that you are equals, yet many do not consider their fellow citizen to be human beings

These humans think of their neighbours as animals, and they treat them — their neighbours — worse than their domestic animals

Often, they appreciate their beasts more than any other human being

This condition has been present throughout the history of humankind until now

Today, you find overexploited, overworked, ill-fed, abandoned, sick, ignored human beings

Man against man

To survive on Earth, you, the Homo sapiens, battled, conquered, and died

On this road, you learned lessons, and though you learned them wrong, you still had to survive, and you did so badly

Your life flows as if carried by a turbulent river that runs through a canyon from the high mountains

You float on the water of life, and you cannot alter its course

You cannot do it

You have control over nothing

You live in dreams without ever stopping, without knowing where you are going

Sometimes, you fall into whirlpools that confound you even more

Worse even, some of you fall into deep abysses that keep

you in fear

You travel through life without ever raising your sight, and the only things you see are these dreadful waters

Sometimes, you can see the walls of rock that pass fast around you, and you may think that there is no end to your predicaments

You may think you cannot escape

When the waters calm and seem not so deep, you are afraid to wade to the shore

You are scared to find other stages, other forms of life

But there are the fortunate ones who can see that the walls that cage the river are not high

They can see that there is a sky beyond the clouds

A wind brings you messages of other lives, other fields, other worlds from other people

And who are those who dare challenge the turbulence of the river?

Who are those who dare climb those walls and uncover what you are, more than what you believe you are?

Around every human body, not within, orbits a plasma microcosm, like a minute star

It is what you call the spirit

When it orbits, it produces a magnetic field that traps the information you provide, which is your lifetime information

Your lifetime information feeds the spirit every millisecond
of your life

It is the fuel the spirit uses to generate energy

This energy controls the gravitational force that keeps the
spirit orbiting around your body

This microcosm of energy involves a community of fundamental principles

These fundamental principles are the essence of what
you are, as human beings, the absolute individuality, the
ego-universality

The spirit is then an incredible technological device
installed in you by The Principle

People's folklore in the western world translates it as "the
breath of God."

Yet, the objective of the spirit is to collect information on
you

The Principle intended to use this information in the next
stage of humans should the experiment have ended as
planned

The spirit is indestructible

It is never sick, and it is not possible to harm it

From the first instant of fertilization and through the period
of formation, like a protecting field, it moves around you

Once you are out of your mother's womb, it keeps around

you through all seasons of your life and until your death
Hence, the embryo already contains a spirit

When you die, the spirit is set free

It begins a long journey to reach the next phase, a more advanced stage of development

This advanced stage of development is what you should strive to get during your lifetime

Life has different seasons

Death has different seasons

The ancient people knew more about it, yet they thought of it as a religious exercise

The soul had to sort out different obstacles to reach a higher status

You talk about purity and perfection

These are virtues about which you have not a clear notion

And because it is difficult to reach these stages in life, you hope to find them in the beyond

You must have explicit knowledge of the meaning of these concepts, but not from a human point of view

Think higher

You must climb to reach a superior level

The spirit is what you are as a person and no more and no

less

The spirit records all that happens in your life

What you see and what you hear, what you remember, what you talk about and what you forget

Like an incredible video camera, the spirit traps everything that has become part of you

This astonishing amount of information, which is your life, is solar dust in space's immensity

The storage of this information is relevant because it will help you continue the road to more advanced life stages

And if humans disappear from the face of the Earth, other civilizations may have the technology to study the long-gone human race

Henceforward, your spirit will be like an open book to them

Keep your life lived to its fullest

Keep your life in balance with yourselves, your neighbours, and the environment

Collect and apply the highest virtues during your lifetime

Feed your bodies and mind with the best you can find

Get rid of what may hurt you and others

What I am saying does not mean that you will earn points to go to the Heavens

Or that you will lose points, and then you will go to Hell

These are medieval concepts that still subsist in times where a fresher promise of life should prevail

Religion, superstition, and imagination have added human attributes to the spirit

Indeed, you have humanized everything spiritual, beginning with God and going down to the base of the pyramid

The Principle inserted this cosmic-plasma field to every creature that came out of the laboratory

By recording every human moment, they aimed to promote humans to an upscale dimension

You must keep in mind and heart that everything you are and everything you have in you is artificial

You are a feat of biological engineering, yet obsolete now

It is in you then, to update yourselves to an unprecedented season of maturity

You must reflect upon the survival of your species

The Principle is but one of many in the infinite vastness of space

Many in deep space have the tools to interpret what is in the spirit

Most of these forces do not want another lifeless planet drifting through deep space

That is why I am here

To talk to you about these things, so you will know who you
are and where you come from

Afterward, where you go is your responsibility

When the individual dies, the spirit is free

Once free of the human body, the spirit does not answer
calls nor receive messages

It does not communicate with a living human

The spirit is essentially human

The arguments that justify its existence are only available in
a living human being

On the nature of the spirit, it is an invisible, independent,
involuntary, sophisticated contraption

This contraption orbits around the human body

Like a swinging door, it opens to the human's inner world
and interstellar space

Sometimes, your body malfunctions, the flow of information switches, and moves in reverse

It now flows from the spirit to the brain, which is like
projecting a film backward

The spirit loses energy, and the body weakens

When this happens, your memories jump without control in
confusing flashbacks

Unsolicited chapters of your life come back to you

Episodes of your life that were, or so you may have thought, forgotten forever

This upsetting, surreal experience affects you

You are then in a constant state of contrasting emotions

You may have critical moments of exhilaration versus severe flashes of sorrow, or you may fall into acute depression, or you may get an unknown illness, a fatal disease — sudden death

Also, for unknown reasons, the spirit abandons its orbit

It flies away from your body without affecting it, and this happens when you sleep and dream; your body may rest, but your brain never does

When your spirit is away, your body remains in a latent mode, and when your spirit returns, you wake up and resume your life

Yet, in extreme cases, your spirit moves away for a longer time

Your body weakens, and you cannot wake up

Your brain loses the connection with the spirit, but the body continues to be alive

Your body still receives the spirit's energy, and although weak, it is enough to keep your body alive

When this happens, your brain and body enter a vegetative state, which may last days, months, or even years

This 'absence of the spirit' may result from severe brain trauma caused by diverse agents

In this case, your brain cannot recover the information contained in the spirit, which is necessary for you to reconnect with your body

In other cases, the spirit moves farther away from the body, and the energy that emanates from it does not reach the body and causes the body to debilitate and die

When the body dies, the spirit moves away toward the infinitude of the cosmos

Hence, as the body needs the spirit's energy, it needs also that of the body

The body's energy generates the gravitation that keeps the spirit circling the body

You, who seek transcendence, understand why you must keep a healthy body
The spirit is sensitive to what is inside you and to what surrounds you

This sensitivity is present every millisecond of your life

It collects all the good, the ugly, the beauty, and the evil that occur to you throughout your life

Nothing is indifferent to the spirit; everything has value, and it rejects nothing

The Earth is a sphere, and your body is a sphere

Hence, your life is a sphere

Everything you do or think comes back to you one way or another, sooner or later

Nobody can escape this condition, not even in dreams

The spirit takes what the body and the mind receives or rejects

The spirit is the net that you as if you were a fisherman, toss and drag through the waters of your entire life

Sometimes you can see this display of energy in a person, which people call the aura

It is usually visible around the head, where most of the energy concentrates

I remind you that in this aura, you can also see the essence of the dominant animal in your body

The spirit is not a property of the individual that shelters it

It belongs to a cosmic network set by The Principle

The spirit has values yet unknown to you

It is to this system that your spirit returns when you die

The spirit is then what you may call the operating system of the human body

An artificial virtual program on which your life runs and connects you with the universe

With the universe, not with nature

And here is the glitch of this program

The Principle did not connect you with nature

It did connect you with the universe

Hence, you do not see the ground where you step on

Your eyes are fixed on the stars above

Yet for the spirit to work well, the mind and the body must be in balance
 It is not the spirit that marks the limit between life and death

What marks the limit between life and death is your mind and your body

Care about your mind and your body, for they are the holiest of temples

Axumeriedes finished his teaching and walked away. People followed him to the city outskirts, then heavy rain fell, people ran to seek shelter, and when they looked back at the road, Axumeriedes was no longer there.

"Axumeriedes threw all my theories overboard," Mr. Lang said to his students.

They sheltered from the rain under a canopy that the military had set for this purpose. There were food and drink and portable toilets there too.

"Axumeriedes is not a deceptive subliminal projection, as you said. Mr. Lang," Paul said. "We all have seen and heard him,"

"It's true, Paul," Sharon said. "Me too. I patted him on the shoulder when he was coming through," and then, turning towards her teacher, "It looks pretty real to me, Mr. Lang."

"You said all of this is a dream that Axumerides is having," Patrick said.

"Yeah, and that we are in his dream," Rachel added.

"He explained all about that, guys," Mary-Jo said.

"Yes, yes," Mr. Lang said. "All of the above are correct, and you will get an A+ for that. But I changed my mind. I had an epiphany, you may say. We all have had an epiphany, an interstellar epiphany, you may name it. It all came to me now, my dear students. Axumeriedes is not dreaming. We are."

"What?"

The students leaned toward their teacher as if he were to reveal them a secret.

"Yes, my young friends," Mr. Lang said. "I think that we are the ones who are dreaming about Axumeriedes. He is the sleeping prophet we all have within. Inside each one of us beats this impulse to learn the truth that pushes to come out, and hardly does. And this is why we want to learn the truth about ourselves, fight injustice, protect nature, and care for the animals. We all want to do that, but it is our civilization that stops us from climbing to the next floor of the house, as Axumeriedes said."

"So, civilization is our enemy, is that what you are saying, Mr. Lang?" Mary-Jo said.

" We have misunderstood civilization's meaning, Mary-Jo, and this is the core of Axumeriedes' teachings. It reflects our dissatisfaction with the way we live."

"Although it doesn't stop us from dreaming, Mr. Lang," Paul said.

"We dream of a better world, Paul, yet, it's that better world that conditions our dreams."

FAREWELL

AXUMERIEDES RETURNED to the first city he visited, the one by the lake where he had landed. The crowd was there, expecting him as if they knew he was coming. Axumeriedes walked through the path that the people opened for him. He reached the lakeshore at the same spot where he had come with the alive fish in his hands. And he turned toward the people, that as the first time of his appearance, crowned the entire beach, and said,

You have heard my words

Leave the Homo sapiens and their ephemeral satisfactions behind

Work hard together to become the Absolute Human

Stop being larvae, and fly like butterflies and seek the fragrant flowers of real knowledge

Do not forget the Seven Sublime Duties

Fulfill them

Follow them to the letter

Do not ever deviate from them

Grow up

Remember who you are

Understand my teachings, and follow them to the letter

Settle the delinquent debt you have with yourselves, the Earth, and the universe

1. Keep the numbers of your population down

2. Keep the sweet water pure

3. Keep the oceans pure

4. Keep the air pure

5. Keep nature pure

6. Keep the Earth's core and atmosphere untouched

7. Keep yourselves pure, living in love and harmony

These were Axumeriedes' last words. He walked among the crowd, his bare feet suspended half an inch or so from the dust. And as people did before, they opened a path for him, and he acknowledged everybody in his way. And as he walked, people closed lines and walked behind him. And there was a multitude following his steps. Axumeriedes reached the lakeshore. He took off the frock, dropped it on the sand, and so, naked as he had come, he entered into the water and waded through it. And as he advanced, his body began gradually to sink as if he were stepping down a submarine set of stairs. And then, the water closed over his head, and the lake was again calm and shining. And a few seconds later, a flash of blinding lightning in the shape of a forked tongue surged upward from the lake, flared up across the clear sky, and kindled the hearts of the people

Made in the USA
Monee, IL
26 March 2021

63932931R00152